RUBY ROSE &
THE CRYSTAL
PALACE

TANYA HADZHIEVA

Disclaimer

This book is designed to provide information and motivation to our readers. It is sold with the understanding that the author and publisher are not engaged to render any type of psychological, legal, or any other kind of medical advice. The content is the sole expression and opinion of its author. Neither the publisher nor the individual author(s) shall be liable for any physical, psychological, emotional, financial, or commercial damages, including, but not limited to, special, incidental, consequential or other damages. Our views and rights are the same: You are responsible for your own choices, actions, and results.

The content of the book is solely written by the author.

DVG STAR Publishing are not liable for the content of the book.

Published by DVG STAR PUBLISHING

www.dvgstar.com

email us at info@dvgstar.com

ISBN: 1-912547-45-7
ISBN-13: 978-1-912547-45-6

WAKE UP WAKE UP CALL

Wake up, wake up call!
Unplug yourself from the rabbit hole.
Should I share the truth?
Or, keep it between me and the Absolute.
It is all a game, they know it too
you are the one who still has no clue.
They programmed us to be slaves,
we should wake up and save ourselves.
How to do this, you may ask?
Stop believing in your daily task.
Your DNA is not junk.
Believe me, I am not drunk.
Use psychedelics and frequencies,
to jump and explore other inner realities.
Once the veil is lifted up,
your awakened soul will lighten up!
Break the mask they told you are,
step and show who you really are.
They play a wicked game of control,
but they cannot have my soul trapped in a goldfish bowl.
Free choice, free will, they say.
That is how they make us obey!
Is it real? Is it fantasy?
Are we living in virtual reality?
Wake up, wake up call!
Stop sleeping, my dear pal!

Tanya Hadzhieva

CONTENTS

No one is you and that is your
power to change your reality!

- Tanya Hadzhieva

ACKNOWLEDGMENTS

This book is dedicated in memory of my grandmother, Radka Bliznakova. She was my best friend, mother, grandmother and the only person that truly believed in me. She even knew that I'd write a book one day. She is my eternal inspiration and will be forever missed. Special thanks to my parents, friends and to my loving boyfriend for supporting me through this journey.

CHAPTER ONE

In The Clouds

"Radka was dead: to begin with."

It is August 12, 2010 when the sun is at its highest peak. Hot waves make the air almost unbearable in the small town of Hadjidimovo, Bulgaria.

Ruby is almost 18 getting ready for her graduation party when something unpredictable happens.

"Hello hello anybody here... Where am I?"

Ruby is bathed in bright white light.

"Am I alive?"

"Yes Ruby, you are more than alive" - the Guardian Angel responds

"Who are you? What is this place? The light is blinding! "You passed out at your grandmother's funeral ceremony. You couldn't bear the loss. We're in your subconscious mind. Your pain brought me here."

"Are you a.. guardian angel?" - Ruby sighs

"Yes, you could say that!" - Guardian Angel whispers

"Why are you here now?" - Ruby asks curiously

"To remind you of your mission. Ruby, you need to be strong. This is just the beginning. You were sent here for a reason."

"My mission?...I feel so lost, I...help me, save my grandmother, angel" - Ruby starts sobbing

"You are stronger than you think Ruby. It is time for you to bring the future into the NOW!"-The voice whispered low into Ruby's ear.

Ruby's appearance is a mixture between her father's grey eyes and her mother's chocolate brown eyes, she has hazel eyes mostly green in bright sunlight, very long wavy dark blonde hair, always worn on a braid, soft pink lips and round face with puffy cheeks. She has a very petite type of body structure, one of a dancer, average height.

Ruby lies unconscious on the floor next to her grandmother's body that has just passed away from a stroke a few hours ago. Radka was more than just a grandmother to Ruby, she meant everything. Ruby tried to save her grandmother as her body was still warm giving false signals to Ruby, before she blacked out. Her mother, Anna is trying desperately to revive her.
"Ruby, Ruby honey, wake up! Please come back to me!"
Ruby's eyes roll, half awake.

"Mother?"

"Yes, honey, I'm here." - Anna sighs with a relief

Anna stroked her daughter's head.

"How long was I out?"- Ruby tried to get up slowly

"Long enough to miss the whole funeral. You know how it goes with all the rituals of saying goodbye to your grandma in the church. Honey, I know your grandmother was your mentor and you were very close, but you need to be able to say goodbye. She would like you to remember her as she was.."

Radka Bliznakova was average height with short, curly dark hair, dark skin and mocha brown eyes. She was never without red lipstick and love in her heart. A real busy bee; she couldn't rest and was always running around caring too much for her family and laughing her wonderfully light laugh. A strong believer of the Christian Orthodox Church, she went every Sunday to pray and respect all celebrations, mostly believing in Christ's teaching of being open-hearted and treating everyone fair with respect.

"She would want you to remember her happy..." said Ruby's mother "...making jokes to cheer her up! Let's remember her like that."

"She died so suddenly," said Ruby "I didn't get to say goodbye. She was my best friend."

Radka used to say that when Ruby was a child, her grandfather brought her to meet her for the first time and as he rode through town with her on the back of the bike she was sure the neighbours would have thought he'd stolen her.

'You were an angel with blond curly hair, pale white skin, pink lips, a tiny nose and only two front teeth when you smiled.' Ruby's grandparents had dark skin, black hair and dark eyes. It still made Ruby laugh to think about her assumed kidnap.

"You should find a hobby. Get creative again."- Anna suggested

3

Anna helped Ruby up, they gathered their things and went home. Exhausted with life and loss, Ruby went straight up to bed.

Sirius B, year of 2121

"How did it go?" asked Celeste

Celeste is a leader of the Galactic Council for Sirius B star. She is also the Crystal Queen residing in the Crystal Palace. The Galactic Council is an intergalactic organization which was created to deal with important matters in the universe, that protects planets from harming each other. Celeste has silver-like shining skin, slim figure, crystal blue eyes, rose-red lips, no hair, only a beautiful crystal crown on top of her head. She was wearing a blue rope. Crystal citizens are far different from the normal bluish skin Sirian species. Crystal city is part of the white dwarf Sirius B. In which peace that has been established for decades is being disrupted and Ruby is their hope to bring balance to life not only on planet Earth but out of space too. She needs to bring future teaching into the now of her timeline.

"I think she is starting to wake up," said Emeralda with a smile

Emeralda is Celeste's daughter also living in the Crystal Palace. She is the Emerald Princess who has a big task to oversee the project on Sirius B and Planet Earth. She possesses different powers that makes her very unique. Emeralda was looking very similar to her mother, but her rope was of course green and her Princess crown was made of Emerald crystals perfectly polished and shiny. Her eyes are also green, not blue like Celeste! The skin and the body structure remains the same, tall, silver-like shiny skin with a very fine figure.

"Good. What about her progress down there? Did she see you?"- Celeste asked with a smile on her face

"No. She thinks I am her Guardian Angel. Her mother brought her round before I could deliver the whole message. I will try again soon, mother"- Emeralda sighs and smiles back to her mother Celeste

"Don't be in a hurry child, when the time is right she will understand everything! Right now she just misses her grandmother. But now we have Radka's magic here we can use it to help Ruby with her mission."- Celeste noted

To my beloved grandma, here I am again bringing you coffee and a cigarette to your grave. Putting flowers in front of the cold stone with your name engraved on it, while tears fall on my cheeks reminding me that I am still alive. Alive to remember and cherish all the memories together. You will forever be my best friend and my inspiration in life. I want you to know that I will always have you in my heart no matter what follows in life. Here I am talking to you hoping you can hear me from above, I have been coming every morning here for months trying to adjust to a reality that I do not want to accept. If you can hear me, I hope to see you in my dreams at least. Do you remember all the times when you used to invite me for dinner so I can walk and stop reading for a bit? I know you and grandpa were worried I would lose my mind and that is why you invited me. I will never forget all the mornings I used to wake up in your house with fresh croissants from the bakery and fresh hot milk from our own cow. This I would always remember, all the care, all the mentoring when I was going through harsh times, you were there for me. You believed in me when no one else did and encouraged me to be strong in life. You were the only one in the family showing interest and care. Deep inside my inner child is desperately looking for this support and attention. I know I need to let you go, but I am not ready yet!

My uncle (your son) is not talking to grandpa anymore, he thinks, grandpa is to be blamed for your death as you were constantly on the move. I remember your life was very harsh grandma. Waking up at 3 am to be at the tobacco field at 4 am to

pick leaves before sunrise and then going to work from 8 am to 5 pm every day with only a slice of bread and some melon for dinner in the summer, staying late till 11 pm every night that is not life. I can only imagine all this hard work in the field. What did it do to your body? Eventually, you will burn out and now that is the result. I'd rather have you still alive now after the villa you worked for so hard is finally done for you two to relax there and now only loneliness is awaiting my grandpa and the rest of us. My life has changed completely since you are gone, I wanted to study to be a doctor and save lives, but now I see doctors didn't save you. I need to change that.

I have to go now grandma life is calling me ...

"Grandma is that you?" Ruby's face burst into a smile "I saw you dying in my dream and then my mother woke me to tell me you were gone. How did I know?"

"We are connected, Ruby. I tried to come to you before I left my physical body. I knew you would be heartbroken. I wanted to prepare you for this transition. I love you so much. I want you to be happy. Remember love is a world on its own and lives in the heart, I will always love you. I also tried with your mum, but you have a connection to the afterlife that one day you will remember and that is why you could see my transition."- Radka explains with worry for Ruby on her face

"I feel lost without your grandma. My parents will never understand me as you do. Are you in Heaven?"- Ruby asked curiously

I also lost trust in the church after you died so suddenly, I don't think God has mercy"- Ruby said with tears dropping on her cheeks.

"My soul is in a good place, don't worry. I want you to focus on your life. You came here for a reason and it is time to let me go. I can see your heart is closing. You mustn't let it, Ruby. We can always meet here, on the astral plane. It is understood that all consciousness resides in the astral plane I will be here to help you when you need me"- Radka asks with a smile

"Grandma... Don't go."- Ruby starts sobbing

"Ruby, Ruby it was just a dream, I've got you. I'm here! Just breathe." Anna held Ruby's trembling body in her arms

"Mum, I dreamt about grandma. No; not about her; of her! It felt so real. We were in this beautiful open cave with a private beach and a waterfall! I lay my head in her lap. I could feel her hands stroking my hair. She was talking to me mum!"

"Oh honey, how wonderful that she came to say goodbye to you! I'm only sorry she didn't pay me a visit"

"I am sure she did pay you a visit, you probably don't remember. Mum, I remember when I was living with grandma and I was very sick, it was winter and grandpa went downstairs with her to create a snowman for me so I could cheer up. I was watching from the window how they did it in the garden. I can say I have been blessed to have such grandparents. They are my idols for a couple.

Anna led her wide-eyed daughter to the kitchen and made them tea and toast for breakfast. There was no way Ruby was going back to sleep now.

"Is dad coming home for my graduation party?"

"Yes, of course! He wants to take you to pick a dress for the celebration and another for your prom! Oh! And we need to pick the venue and choose the menu for your party too!"

Ruby's eyes filled with tears. She didn't feel like celebrating anything at all.

"Nothing matters now she's gone." she said, remembering how her grandmother longed to see her graduate "Can we cancel the party? I'm sure people will understand"

"Let's talk about this another time." said Anna "Right now I think we could both do with a nice long walk."

"Emeralda, did you do your homework?" said Celeste, peering down at her daughter

"Yes, mum. I connected with all 50 crystals! Why am I not supposed to know about Moldavite?"

"It is not the right time."
Emeralda scowled a little

"Did you see how Ruby's grandmother impacts her life, even in the dream state? A truly incredible connection."
"Can I play outside with the flowers today?" Emeralda asked

"You can, but don't forget to keep an eye on Ruby! Can you also pick some roses I would like to take a healing bath with them?"

In the Crystal city everything is made of crystals, even flowers. Their healing power is used by crushing them into a powder mixed with water for a healing bath or they can be taken internally as a medicine!

Ruby was devastated after losing her one and only foundation in life, feeling like an angel with broken wings the last thing she wanted to do was celebrate. She spent the whole time after her grandma's death until her graduation party in

isolation. Almost not eating, sitting in a dark room with a very sad song's playlist trying to figure it out in her mind, what went wrong. Where Ruby was born is not popular to see a counsellor for grieving, you are labelled as weak if you cannot go through it by yourself. Ruby made sure she was occupied with art, writing and studying English to get her mind off the sudden loss. Time for celebration has come and Ruby needs to face her fears of being in the spotlight.

"Come out Ruby everybody wants to see you in the dress!" Anna yelled in excitement

"Voila!" Ruby appeared in a long silk chameleon dress that changed from grey to violet as she moved. "What do you think?"

The whole room turned to look at Ruby. Her hair fell to her waist in Barbie curls and was decorated with sequins. Her bright grey sparkly high-heels matched her purse.

"Allow me to escort you to the car Madame." said her cousin Angel

Everyone waited outside to take pre-prom pictures with Ruby. She was excited. Her whole family was there to support her. She really didn't expect so many people to turn up for the party; even cousins from far-off cities came to see her.

"Only one person is missing" Ruby whispered to her mother

"Ruby this is your moment. You are 18 and your life has just begun. Graduating from high school is only one part of it. I told you they would give you the white gloves at school. You deserved it. You were an excellent student." Anna smiled at her daughter, all grown up.

"I really didn't expect to get the white gloves mum. Usually, it's the teacher's children who get picked! I never thought they'd notice my achievements"

Only excellent students get to receive such honors as white gloves upon graduation.

"We are very proud of you honey!" said Ruby's father "You have been the best daughter. We couldn't have asked for more!"

Ruby knew how hard her father had worked to send her to an English private school. She thanked him from the bottom of her heart and gathered her family to take photographs of the special day. She only saw her dad once or if lucky twice a year as he was always working abroad to be able to provide food and a roof for the family. He still cries when thinking for all the years he missed of Ruby's life and what she has become.

CHAPTER TWO

Leaving The Nest

"Dad, are you ready?" Ruby shouted up the stairs "We need to go! My University tour is this afternoon! And we need to drop my stuff in the apartment first!"

"Alright, alright!" Ruby's father George said, hauling bags down the staircase "I'm ready! I just need to take the bags to the car. Your mother is staying home; you have so many suitcases we can't fit her in! the car."

Ruby was excited to start a new chapter. She kissed her mother goodbye and joked about not making friends

"You know me! Always the outsider" she said, nervous that it might be true.

Anna waved goodbye to her daughter.

As Ruby and George pulled away, Ruby turned to her father and asked him a question. She rarely saw him and now he was a captive audience she longed for a conversation to hold on to while she was away from him.

"Dad, what's your fondest memory of me? The most memorable moment?"

"Why do you ask?"

"It's a long drive..." said Ruby, crossing her hands in an attempt at nonchalance.

"Haha, well there are a few!" said George, a smile creeping across his face "I remember when we caught you smoking in eighth grade. You set a whole bush alight trying to hide it!"

"And then you locked me in a room and blew smoke in my face for hours so I'd hate the smell forevermore!" said Ruby

"Well, it worked didn't it?!"

Ruby smiled.

"Ruby, I am sorry I have been away so much. So often. Maybe you will understand when you have a family to look after" said George quietly "But I have more memories of you than you think- I was with you a lot when you were little"

"You know when I miss you the most, Dad? When I'm sick!" said Ruby "I always worry I might wake up one day and never see you again." Her eyes filled with tears.

"Your grandma's death really got to you didn't it?" said George softly

The car trundled over the crumbling motorway.

"I'm here now," he said

When they eventually arrived and opened the car door, the reflective calm of the car snapped into bustle and action as Ruby shoved her suitcases into her room and hurried down to start the tour.

"Here we are Ruby, this is your new home! A new life! Go and explore!" George smiled at his daughter as she ran off into the next chapter.

"See you soon dad!" yelled Ruby, bounding into the future.

As she approached the meeting room, the butterflies kicked in.

"Good afternoon students. You will be given a guided tour the university and then your teachers will explain the program for the first year of studying Applied Linguistics"

"I think Ruby is ready to receive her power!" said Emeralda, bounding toward her mother.

"She's developing, definitely, but I am not quite sure she is ready for the first wave of transfusion! What do you think, Koral?"

"I think we should give it a go and see how she reacts!" said Koral, throwing his arms up "We'll wait until she goes to sleep, then Emeralda will connect and then, transfer the power!"

Koral was the right hand of the Queen, a warrior sworn to defend the kingdom! He was always ready for a fight, his battle clothing with a sword on his left side spoke out loud. He is very handsome with a very well-built body and a diamond smile!

"It will be done tonight, mother!" yelped Emeralda excitedly. "Do you also want me to teach her how to use it as well?"

"Yes, Emeralda"- she will be your warrior to train.

Emeralda was waiting for the perfect timeline on planet Earth to make the transfusion. The process consists of channelling high-frequency energy vibe from The Ether and channelling it to a person, in this case, Emeralda was going to touch a crystal quartz with one hand to amplify the frequency being used and with her other hand, she would touch her 3rd eye.

Ruby had met a lovely girl on the tour and when they found out they'd be living together they couldn't believe their luck. They both had the same interests in arts, yoga and nature. It turns out Mary is a cousin of Ruby's best friend from home.

"Hi Mary, I am so excited I will be living with you. We share so much in common. I know you are more into arts so maybe you can give me some tips?" Ruby asked with a smile on her face.

"Yes, of course, Ruby. I will be happy to help. I am also very excited I have heard my cousin talking about you a lot, but never imagined I would meet you and live together. She will be probably very jealous when I tell her. Which bed do you like more?"

"I would rather have the bed next to the window, thank you for asking. You are so kind! Shall we unpack and get some sleep, it was a very busy day for both."

It was a chilled night in September when the clock was showing 11:11 pm as Ruby felt a sharp pain going down her right side from head to toe.

"What is it Ruby?" said Mary, sitting bolt upright

"Ouch! It hurts! It's burning!... Mary! Help me!" Ruby yelled, trying to get up but instead she fell over "Call an ambulance I don't know what's going on. It feels like I've pinched a nerve- my whole right side feels like it's on fire!" Ruby cried

"911 What is your emergency?"

"Please come fast my friend is in a lot of pain. She can't even stand up, she is laying on the floor. She thinks is a pinched nerve."

"We will be there in 5 min, please do not move the patient!- the medic replies

"Mary can you open the door I think I can hear the doorbells ringing I am sure it's the medical team."

"Good evening. Can you please rate the pain you are experiencing and from 1 to 10 and what is the feeling like?"- the medic asks

"The pain is 10 I cannot move and my nerve feels like a pulled string on a guitar. I need some medication to make it relax, please."

"I will give you an injection which will help with the pain, but please see a doctor tomorrow and they need some x-rays to see what is the problem".- the medic responds

"I will, please make it go away for now! Can you help me to get back into bed?" Ruby requested

"This is all we can do for now. Hope you feel better and please see a doctor. Good night girls, if it gets worse please dial 911 again" the medic said

"Ruby do you need anything?"
"No, Mary, thank you! I think the medication is starting to work now! I will try to go to sleep. You should too."

"Well, Emeralda that did not go as planned." said Celeste "What happened?"

"I don't know mum, I must have given her too much energy?

Maybe more than her body could hold..?" Emeralda replied

"Or she wasn't ready," said Koral sternly

"Well that was your idea wasn't it?!" snapped Celeste "I knew the body wasn't ready. You cannot compare Earth years to ours. Her body will always remember this pain, Merlin. Now it is stored in her cellular memory!"

"We'll find a way to improve her health. We always do. I'll study and connect to more crystals!" said Emeralda, searching for a solution.

"Well, keep us updated. For now, we will keep an eye on her. No more experiments."

"Hi, Mary! How are you?"

Ruby hadn't seen Mary for about 3 years, not since they lived together at university. Ruby had lived on her own since university

"Of course it's pricier when you're not sharing bills, but you know me!" joked Ruby

"I sure do! How is your leg? Does it still bother you?" Mary asked

"Only when my immune system is low. How's life? Are you going away to work for the summer?"

"No, I will stay in Bulgaria. What about you? Are you going to the States again?"

Yep! Third time lucky!" Ruby laughed

"Why don't you just stay there?" said Mary

"Oh, you know my mum. She can't survive two weeks without me! She is barely making it through the summers." Ruby replied, knowing that she couldn't live this way forever.

"Do you think about the uni days much? What do you remember most?"

"Not a lot, to be honest. I feel like it was a waste of time really. I didn't learn much more than what I already knew from the private school." said Ruby "Mostly, I remember my bad luck with relationships. How about you?"

"About the same. But I enjoyed the clubs a lot!" Mary laughed.

"Hello?" Ruby picked up her phone "Who's this?"

"It is Ellie from the agency, your visa has just arrived and your sponsor confirmed. You are going to Maine, USA."

"Oh my God!" Ruby nearly jumped in the air "I am so excited. Thank you, Ellie. I'll pack my stuff and stop by at the office to collect my visa!"

Ruby could barely contain her excitement as she dialled 'Home'.

"Mum, guess what? I just got accepted to go to the USA again" Ruby gabbled.

Anna was silent.

"Aren't you happy for me?" said Ruby

"Yes, of course, I am honey," said Anna "When are you coming home to pack? Shall I call your dad to come home from Spain to say goodbye?"

"Yes, please call him! I'll see you in 2 days! Bye, mum!"

Anna called her husband and made a grand plan to celebrate Ruby's departure over the Easter weekend.

Easter weekend came and Ruby and Anna had been preparing the food all day.

"Mum! Mum! We need to go and get dad from the station! It's nearly time!" said Ruby, impatient to see her father after nearly two years.

"Yes alright Ruby! I'm just getting dressed, give me a minute! If you're ready, you can start the car. You're the one with a driving license!" Anna laughed

"I'm giving you 5 minutes then I'm leaving without you!"

At the bus station, Ruby threw herself into her father's arms and told him excitedly about all the preparations they'd made for the weekend. They decided they'd go straight to Ruby's godmother's.

"Are we going to the late night mass after dinner?" said David

"We can of course but that depends of how drunk you guys are planning to be" Ruby replied

"Well honey, you know I don't drink much, so it'll be up to your dad" said Anna, arching an eyebrow.

"Ruby! Can you please come and help me cut the cake!" asked Elena, Ruby's godmother.

"Coming!" Ruby walked into the kitchen and looked back at her family "Look at them! I never thought I'd see my dad dancing!"

"Are we going to church? It's almost midnight," said Elena

Ruby called her family off the living room dance floor and they headed out into the night.

"Ruby, I need to talk to you?" George said, huddling alongside her

"What's up..?" said Ruby, smelling alcohol on her father's breath "Are you drunk? You smell a lot like alcohol. How much did you drink? I'm not sure you can go to church like that"

"I had to have a drink. I wouldn't have the strength to tell you this otherwise." said George gravely "I have done something wrong by you, but the longer I keep it a secret, the worse it gets."

"Spit it out, dad. You are scaring me."

"I want to ask your mother for a divorce. I've been living with another woman in Spain for three years and I'm in love with her. I'm so ashamed I kept it a secret for so long- I just did not know how to tell you and how to make it right" Ruby's father burst into tears.
"Oh my God, I don't know what to say. For the first time in my life I am speechless. I can't believe this." said Ruby, searching "That's why you didn't want me to come and see you in Spain or apply to colleges there! All this time it was because of a woman,! Poor mum. She thinks everything is fine and that she'd move there too! How can you be telling me this now, on this wonderful occasion and days before I leave for the states? Could you not have picked a better time? If there is any..." Ruby couldn't continue and started sobbing uncontrollably.

"I am sorry honey, I am really sorry!"

"Leave me alone!" Ruby said, pushing her father away "You have to tell her. I can't do this for you!"

In the church, after circling three times and celebrating the resurrection of Christ, Ruby stayed behind. When she knew she was alone she knelt at a pew and prayed.

"Dear Angel,

Hear my prayer.
My life is crumbling under my feet;
You took my grandma and now my family is falling apart;
Please give me the light and guidance to know what to do now.
I feel lost- my foundations in life have been taken away.
Have I wronged God so much that I am being put through all of this suffering to pay the price?
On this bright night and celebration of Christ, give me the strength to continue and to fulfil my destiny. Please angel, guide me through my spiritual journey. Amen."
As Ruby left the church she knew it was time to leave her hometown for good. She wouldn't feel at home now her home was broken. Now the whole world would be her home.

"Welcome to America Ruby I am your sponsor Carole, I'll be taking care of you while you're here."

Carole was a very short lady in her 60s that drove cautiously and what Ruby considered to be uncomfortably close to the wheel. She was not what Ruby had imagined at all but she seemed kind.

"I appreciate you picking me up from the airport! When do I start work? Tomorrow morning?" said Ruby, keen as ever to start the next adventure.

"Wow, you're keen!" Carole replied "But, yes, you can start tomorrow if you like?"

"Let's just say I'd like to keep busy right now"

Maine was beautiful. There were flowers everywhere and Ruby could smell the sea air, even from the window of the car.

"We hope you feel comfortable in a shared house." said Carole "We have 4 girls arriving tomorrow from China. They will be working in another department, but living in the same house as you. We hope you don't mind"

"No, of course not" said Ruby, glad at the thought of company "I will make sure to get my bearings before they arrive so I can show them around!"

The house was enormous. Ruby had the pick of the rooms and threw herself onto the nearest bed. "Oh my God! This is the best bed I've ever tried! The mattress feels like a cloud!"
"I'll leave you to it!" Carole called "See you tomorrow morning at seven. You'll be helping us with setting up breakfast, lunch, and dinner!"

Every day for the next six months Ruby worked for Carole, serving breakfast, serving lunch and serving dinner at the hotel. Just as the monotony was getting to Ruby, something happened.

As she lay in bed one night, a huge ball of bright light woke her. She heard an unidentifiable voice coming from somewhere.

"Ruby, Ruby wake up! I have a message for you!" the voice said "You are almost ready for your task. To prepare yourself you must study spiritual practices. Start with yoga and crystals! It is vital for your personal development!"

Then, just like that, the voice disappeared.

Ruby ended up staying in Maine for three years longer than the six months she'd planned. She secretly translated all her diplomas from Bulgaria and applied for college there where she graduated with an Associate's degree in Liberal Arts. She made a lot of friends from a lot of different countries and had some not so successful relationships. Her father never realised the trauma he caused and the impact it had on Ruby- especially in her love life. In fact, she barely spoke to her father now but talked to her mother every day to make sure she was alright. Her mother ended up getting nothing from the divorce and was even told to leave the house because George's sister would not allow her to stay. Now her mum was living with relatives in another town. When Ruby's grandfather got sick, Ruby knew it was time to go home.

CHAPTER THREE

Safe Haven

Ruby screamed with happiness when she saw her mother at the arrivals gate. They held each other tight, in the way that people do at airports, and talked over each other.

"I am so happy you're back" cried Anna "Those 3 years were the worst of my life! I missed you so much! I am sure we have a lot to talk about!"

"Mum, I have so much to tell you. A lot of things have happened to me and some of them may come as a shock! Let's just go home. We can talk then."

At home, Anna made them tea and cut the coffee cake she had especially for Ruby's homecoming.

"So honey, tell me all about it! I want to know everything!" said Anna, handing Ruby her cup

"Mum, a lot happened to me while I was in the states. Work was work, but since grandma passed away, I have been having some very vivid dreams. I think they are telling me to start learning more about... spirituality"
"Don't tell me you've joined some kind of cult Ruby!"

23

"No, mum, no. I started studying yoga and crystals. In the beginning it was to see if I could heal myself. But now it's more than that. I also started studying Numerology and Astrology and even Human Design!"

"Wow Ruby" said her mother, "I am completely in shock. I would have never thought you'd be interested in that. You were more of a make-up, high heels and clubs kind of girl...I hardly recognise you!"

"Well, this is who I am now and you will have to accept that I have changed!" said Ruby bluntly

"Did anything interesting happen, apart from you becoming a hippy?" Anna half-joked

"Yes" said Ruby, "I met a very special person there that was my best friend, partner and mentor"

"You never told me you had a boyfriend in the USA?" said Anna "Was he treating you well?"

"Yes mum."

"I'd like to hear about him," said Anna. Ruby seemed distracted so Anna changed the subject for now "So tell me about these vivid dreams... did you see grandma again" she said.

"It was more like I was receiving messages about what I needed to do next. Call it sixth sense. But the books were calling me. I remember when our whole class from college went to the Boston Arts Museum and I was just drawn into this enormous Buddha store nearby. That's where I bought my first book about spirituality. After that, one thing just flowed into the next."
"Sounds addictive" replied Anna cautiously.

"Once you realise how much more there is than the physical body it can be addictive!" said Ruby, seemingly oblivious to her mother's concern

"But now let me tell you about Rob. I'm sorry I didn't mention him before. After I left the job at Carole's hotel, I started working at a smoothie bar. One day this guy was staring at me while he was having lunch. He was wearing dark sunglasses but I could still tell where his eyes were and I was wondering what the hell he wanted from me! When he finished eating he came straight up to me and asked me what the best smoothie was. "The peanut butter bliss" I replied, "With a shot of coffee to freshen you up." I mean, he'd just eaten; he couldn't have wanted a smoothie; he just wanted an excuse to come and talk to me! He bought one anyway and we started talking about spirituality- he'd noticed I was wearing a necklace with an Om sign- the sign of the universe. "So you like yoga, do you also meditate?" he asked. I told him I was planning to sign up for a certification in Maine and asked him if he practiced too. "Yes" he said "I am planning to go to India and get certified there. Would you like to come?" So then he gave me the website of the place he was considering and said

"Also this is my number if you would like to hang out sometime."

"So, did you guys end up seeing each other for a long time?" Anna asks

"Well, yes, we did for almost a year, but then I came back" said Ruby

"Is he handsome, tell me all about your relationship"- Anna asks impatiently

"As I was living with a very narcissistic family back then it looked like I was trapped in a high tower and he was the prince that rescued me. Very handsome. Tall, very well-built body. Same hair dark blond as me and same hazel eyes. People thought I was his daughter, the resemblance was uncanny. We were texting back and forth for weeks which was also very synchronized, but then the invitation for the first date came along which was amazing. He even remembered I like books, so he gave me a book as a present. It was called The Time Traveller's Wife. I remember clearly, the night, the book, everything. Then he would come to see me at work in the winter with his motorcycle. Which was madness as it was so cold in Maine during winter I cannot imagine biking. He came just to give me a love card sprayed with his cologne so it can remind me of him. During the weekends is when we can only meet so I would stay at his place and we will go and explore restaurants and nature that is around. We even went to a spring every Sunday to pour water into a glass jug full of crystals inside. The crystals charge the water especially when you leave it on the sunlight as well. I would always record any synchronicity happening during our conversation in the car. Sometimes it was just too much. We also did yoga together and he taught me how to read tarot cards for the first time. This is where my spiritual development started with all the new books you see at home now. But of course, it was not meant to be for us to be together. The big difference was age and it did separate us as we wanted different things from life. We are still great friends. I remember he used to say:' "You are a multifaceted diamond, all your facets are different and they are all beautiful." "So here it is my story in short, mum!"

"Woow I am shocked, Ruby! That is an amazing story, it touched me very much. I am sure you will find someone your age that can share the same values and same interests very soon. I wish it from my heart!"

"Thanks mum. I am still getting over it. I know I will eventually move on and get a life, but for now, please no more questions."

Ruby decided to stay in Bulgaria for the summer and see if it will work out. Anna had a new boyfriend who made an excellent breakfast.

"Come and join us I have made breakfast" said Pascal, as Ruby came downstairs one morning

"Mm, it smells good! I would love to try some French toast" said Ruby, dolloping homemade jam onto her plate.

"Ruby, I saw an advertisement for a job in a hotel nearby" said Pascal, handing Ruby the paper "Let me know if you want me to come with you and check it out."

"Sure, let's go down after breakfast!"

Pascal went upstairs to get ready and left mother and daughter alone.

"Mum, is Paskal always so serious?" said Ruby "And tell me he treats you well or I'll…"

"He is great" Anna replied "You'll see. He's actually very funny!"

In the car Paskal asked Ruby about the USA, he wanted to hear all about it from her, not from Anna. Ruby told him about all the pros and cons, about meeting Rob and her decision to come home when her grandfather got sick.

"Well, you're here now" said Paskal "And I'm so glad. I want you to feel at home. My house is your house."

"Rise and shine sweetheart!" called Anna "Come and join us at the table! The sun is up and we are planning a hike! Do you want to come?"

"Yes I'd love to!" said Ruby "Oh wow, what a spread! Mum did you make all of this?"

Ruby got stuck into her favourite coffee cake and some

freshly brewed tea. There were homemade jams and a big bowl of fruit- they were going to be ready for this hike. When Paskal left the room to get ready Ruby took the opportunity to talk to her mum.

"I'm thinking about starting a job soon, but if I don't like it..." said Ruby cautiously "Maybe I should go abroad again?"

"Are you sure honey? You just got back? You don't have to start working until you feel ready. I know you feel certain pressure from Pascal, but I assure you he means well" said Anna, hoping her daughter would stay.

"Thanks, mum. I really appreciate your support. Did you see all the books and crystals I brought back from the states?"

"I saw some rocks on your desk, is that what you mean by 'crystals'?" said Anna curiously. "What do they do?"

"They have a healing power. I have a book on how to use them."

"Wow, Ruby. Do you really believe in these things? I mean they are not scientifically proved, are they? I just don't want you to get a false hope" Anna said, concerned.

"You don't need to worry about me. I knew people here would not be prepared for all this. You know, sometimes, I see how to use them in my dreams. But you're the first person I've shared about it.

"Thank you for sharing honey." said Anna "Go and get dressed. We are going on this hike soon!"

"Are we all ready with water, food and proper clothes" Paskal asked

"Yes, I think we are ready Paskal. Now, Ruby, the hike will be six hours round trip- are you ready for this?" asked Anna

"I have done it before mother, why are you doubting me now?! Hold on I just want to grab my crystals for my meditation later." said Ruby, running upstairs.

"Shall we stop for a bit of a break?" said Anna after an hour and a half "I want to smoke a cigarette."

"Mother, smoking is bad for you." scolded Ruby "That's why you are out of breath. But if we are stopping I'm going to meditate here on the side of the trail. Just let me know when we are leaving."

"Ok honey, we'll rest for fifteen minutes, grab something to eat and then we'll press on!" said Anna

For her meditation Ruby always used an Om track. She laid down on the grass, put her headphones in and started listening.

"Ruby, Ruby can you hear me?" Ruby wasn't hearing Om but the voice that came to her as she slept that night years ago

"Who are you? Why can I hear you in my head? I'm not even asleep!" Ruby looked around confused

"Your meditation has opened a door for us to connect. I'm your 'guardian angel' remember? I've been watching over you for a long time!" Emeralda replied

"Why are you watching over me? Have I done something wrong?" Ruby asked

"No, on the contrary. You are a magical soul, Ruby. You have a very important task in this lifetime. I would like to give you this tattoo. I will place it in the middle of your forehead, on top of your third eye. It will be invisible to the naked eye... so no need to worry about your parents" Emeralda said with a twinkle

"What is the purpose of this tattoo?" said Ruby

"This is a way we bond and can connect more easily. If you ever need me just put a crystal over it and the connection will be restored. Now, I need to tell you a secret, Ruby. Are you ready?"

"Yes, your secret is safe with me!"

"You are a Crystal Citizen. You are a healer, Ruby!" said Emerelda "You have been sent to bring peace. Power lies within you. You can learn to channel it though your hands, eyes or any part of your physical body. Do you understand?"

"I'm what? As far as I am concerned, I live in Bulgaria, planet Earth. I'm just a human being, there must be a mistake."

"Try to focus Ruby" said Emeralda "We are running out of time. Your time to heal others and bring peace will come very soon"

"Is that why I am attracted to crystals?" said Ruby

"It is in your soul contract, you chose to come here to help humankind ascend to a higher level of consciousness!"

"Why do I not remember anything of this soul contract you speak of?"

"If you knew the answers of a test everything would be too easy. It will all come together trust me. We are here to support you with this transition. I can help with training you to gain control of your power. All you need to do is put a crystal on your forehead and connect with me when you are ready."

"We..?" said Ruby. But before the question could be answered, her mother's voice came through.

"Ruby, Ruby.. let's go honey!"

Ruby slowly opened her eyes, adjusting to the new environment.

"What just happened to me?" said Ruby in a daze

"What honey, are you talking to me?" Paskal asked

"No, no I am talking to myself! I'll be fine. I just need five more minutes,please!"

"That is fine! Take your time!" Paskal replied

"Anna are you sure Ruby is ok? She seems a bit strange today." Paskal whispered to Anna "Do you think it's the time zone change?

"I feel the same, but I haven't said anything- I don't want to offend her" Anna replied

"I am ready to go, guys. I'm sorry. It was meditation that made me a bit dizzy!" Ruby said as she reappeared on the path.

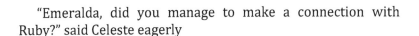

"Emeralda, did you manage to make a connection with Ruby?" said Celeste eagerly

"Yes, mother I did. I gave some of the information you requested. I told her that she is a healer. But I didn't tell her everything. We don't want to overwhelm her.

"There is a lot of pressure from the Federation of The Galaxy to raise human consciousness and you have signed up for this. We do need to speed up the process. Do everything in your power to get her out of Bulgaria. This is not the country for her development. We need her to wake up fully soon." said Celeste

31

"I know the rules mother, but I remember when we first tried to channel the information- her nervous system broke down. It wasn't good for her body or her mind."

"You have one mundane year to finish the job, Emeralda. I am your mother, but I also have responsibilities as a Leader of the tribe here on Sirius B. I trust it will go well and you will train Ruby to become a warrior on earth by connecting to her true essence of the Crystal Palace.

"How do you like the hike so far, Ruby?" said Paskal

"I love it. The lake is beautiful. Crystal clear cold water! I might put my feet in and see if those fish will come to me."

"Do it!" said Paskal. Ruby was starting to see his fun side. "I will be by your side just in case. They'll want to eat your dead skin so be prepared!" Pascal laughed.

Coming back to Bulgaria was great for Ruby in some ways. She got to reconnect with family and feel the love she was missing in the USA. After six months working in a hotel, Ruby decided to leave Bulgaria; this time for the UK.

"Mum, I am going away again; but this time I know you are not alone. You have Pascal and my little baby Ciara. Take care of my cat. She loves you too. I will try to make it work better this time. I know you hate me being away, but trust me; I have a good feeling about this one."

"Ruby, I will always miss you when you are away from me. One day, when you are a mother too, you will understand. Please come back to see us from time to time. We wish you the best of luck." Anna tried not to cry, but she was welling up. Pascal stepped in "If you need us, we will always be here. And if things get difficult, please come home, Ruby"

"Goodbye" Ruby whispered back

Ruby was astonished when she reached London. It was quite a shock once she had landed and realised what a small world she had been living in back home. She came from a village, so London seemed vast at first. She spent 6 months working as a cleaner and interpreter in hospitals, schools and courts to make a living- and hated her life. She was on the edge of giving up and returning home - she couldn't believe that despite all her diplomas and awards, she had to put up with such a life.

One day when she was walking down the street, she felt a sharp pain in her abdomen. Ruby had six stones in each kidney. Ruby was miserable; no home, no partner, no family, no stable job...

"Hi honey, how is life in London? We haven't heard from you for a while... Are you happy?"

"Hi mum. I'm alright. I have been struggling with kidney stones; I think I will come home for a bit. I can't seem to recover properly"

"Oh no! I used to get them, and your grandfather as well. I am sorry to hear that Ruby. I know it hurts, but come home I will take care of you!"

"I am buying a ticket for next week. I hope I recover fast- I want to go up to the lakes."

Ruby felt constantly bombarded by other people's projections: She was feeling guilty that she had failed again after returning from the USA. She was so sure that this trip would be a success. Her mum seeing her as a failure was what really bothered her; and kept in the UK. She wanted to prove she was worthy of recognition. Ruby was a stranger in a foreign country trying to make a living; and this fast-paced, stressful life was damaging her health. On top of that, she had lost the only person that made her feel worthy; the only person that she didn't have to prove anything to; her grandma.

Dear Grandma,

I know you look after me from above, so hear me out!
I cannot hold on to life alone. The days seem so long and I'm so lonely.
I feel lost in this big city, not knowing anyone. You know me; I have simple values. All I want is a heart I can trust. A heart that will beat next to mine. I suffer because I am in conflict with myself. It seems ages since I last spoke to you, but this feels like a crossroads.

Guide me, please! I need you more than ever!

With Love,
Your Granddaughter

Sirius B, 2121

Emeralda asked the family to gather and discuss the next steps for Ruby. They can see she is struggling. Their main concern is that the physical body seems strong, but her mind is weakening. They needed to take action, and fast.

"Emeralda, tonight is very important!" said Celeste "You will meet with Ruby again and tell her more of what she is; she needs to know, and believe in herself. The image is your choice, you can go to her as her grandma or yourself. Either way, tonight is the night."

"Yes, mother. It will be done"- Emeralda replied

CHAPTER FOUR

Revelation

On her first night back home, Ruby laid in bed exhausted and in pain after her long journey. After an hour or so, the painkillers she took started to work, and she began to doze off.

"Who's there?"

"Hi, Ruby. It's me Emeralda. Do you recognize me?"

Emeralda stood smiling in front of her.

"Hold on. I've seen you before. You look like me when I was a child. With gold curly hair, green eyes and sandy skin. Except your skin sparkles and shines as if you were made of diamonds."

"Ruby, remember when I told you you have a power; that you can help other people feel better? Your presence is healing and draws people that need you into your life. You are a magnet and people will want to drain your energy; but you are here to do way more than heal. Follow me, I want to show you something", said Emeralda. Emeralda started simulating an experience for Ruby in the astral plane. "We are currently on Sirius B; what humans would understand as a 'white dwarf.' But Sirius B is more than that. We live in Crystal City. It serves as a powerhouse; to provide healing to other planets in the galaxy. That is why we need to keep it pure. Imagine that we are the pharmacy that everyone visits when they get sick.

"I see that everything here is made of crystals" said Ruby "But what does have to do with me?"

"Ruby, you are part of me- and- I am you..."

Ruby looked very confused.

"Wait a minute, I need to recap a bit. Did you just said I am you?" she said

"Ok, I will explain in full." said Emeralda with a chuckle "I was born as Emeralda here in the Crystal Palace on the star Sirius B. At the time of my birth my soul split in two. Now, this is a rare event; but it can happen. It's a soul contract. The other part of my soul is in you, Ruby. That is why we are ONE. You and I are living parallel lives. One on Planet Earth and one here.

"This is not real, is it? It's all just a dream. It can't be true! I am just Ruby. Just Ruby." Ruby said with her mouth open

"Ruby, you are so much more. Your body, mind and soul are capable of so much more. You are connected to other dimensions simultaneously. That's why you see people dying in your dreams; before their physical death. It's easy for you to connect with their spirit when it is due to depart. This is a gift. Your sensitivity and pure heart are a gift to humanity. Your ability to heal people is not only within your hands; you can channel healing frequencies from any part of your body." said Emeralda

"If I am a healer, why am I suffering from kidney stones?" Ruby asked

"Ruby, your physical body suffers as a result of your mental state; you have been living in agony and stress for a long time - your body is trying to resolve it for you. We will help you with the healing process, but you need to focus. We need to work together. Remember we are ONE."

"Does this mean I could have saved my grandmother?"

"Interfering with free will is not what we do. You can help those that need you and you will recognise them; they will invite you into their lives so you can guide them through the healing process. Every soul signs a contract and when they are done, there is nothing you can do; it's just time for them to go. Most people die prematurely as they have not resolved conflicts that have been passed onto them though their ancestral DNA memory. At conception, all the DNA transfers the information, including the trauma, that needs to be resolved in this current life."

Emeralda was pleased with her explanation; Ruby was starting to understand.

"I am shocked" Ruby said "But it is starting to make sense to me. When I was little I would always dream of my relatives dying; and remember my last conversation with them. I understand I have powers, but what am I supposed to do with them? What is my mission? Can you guide me?"

"Yes, Ruby of course. I would like to introduce you to my, well our, mother; Celeste. She is the Crystal Queen of our city and a member of the Galactic Council."

"Hi, Ruby" Celeste smiled at her "It is so nice to finally meet you. We have so much to catch up on as you are ready now!

"Celeste? All your names are crystals too! What does yours mean?" Ruby was excited. She was starting to feel at home with these beings.

"Well" said Celeste "Allow me to tell you a story. Everyone that is born here, is born with a certain energetic frequency, that determines their name and the destiny they carry. The energy I carry is of a crystal called Celestite. It is used for Angelic communication and accessing higher dimensions, as well as aiding serenity and forgiveness. It is my mission to channel this frequency to other worlds, and to hold that energy in our city so we maintain balance. All of us are educated on what the different names and frequencies mean, by focusing our minds. We can read anything without speaking. Speaking is an Earth only matter, as humans have not yet evolved to telepathically communicate. But it is in you; you have the ability to do it and Emeralda will show you."

"What does my name mean mum?" asked Ruby

"Ruby , Ruby, you are waking up...

"Ruby, Ruby" said Anna with a smile "Wake up honey. I've made your favourite! French toast with homemade jelly. Why don't you join me and Paskal in the kitchen? You need to get your strength back."

"Good morning mother. I had a very profound dream last night. I'll join in a minute, just give me time to fully wake up."

Ruby's doctor said that her Magnesium and Vitamin D levels were depleted, so Anna took her out in the sun for 3 hours every day to make sure she ate well; preparing food with the right nutrients for Ruby's recovery. The two-week retreat home had Ruby looking like new; a smile back on her face and a sparkle in her eye. Being close to her family and her lovely cat, that slept with her every night, kept the positive vibe going. Hiking in the mountains and being close to the lakes brought Ruby's spirit back. Knowing what she now knew from the meeting with her twin soul Emeralda, she was in a better state to keep moving forward.

"Ruby, what movie would you like to watch tonight? Let's get some popcorn and put on a nice movie before bed." Paskal suggested

Watching a movie together was like a reunion after a long day.

"I'd love to. Let's watch The Spy! It's a great comedy - lifts your spirits!." Ruby answered

"I have a headache. I don't think watching a movie is a good idea for me" Anna replied

"You're overworked, that's why. I saw you spent all day in the garden without a break. I have an idea, lie down I will do a healing for you with my hands" said Ruby

Her mother obediently laid down on the bed with her eyes closed. Ruby spread her hands across her mother's body, channelling frequencies from other dimensions and clearing the aura blockages that may have caused the headache. After 20 minutes of full relaxation Anna woke up and felt completely new.

"How was it mum?" Ruby was curious to know how she had done

"It was amazing. I felt like I was floating on a cloud and no more headache! How did you do that?" Anna asked

"I told you I have special powers. Are you ready for the movie now?"

"Yes, let's watch! I'll grab the popcorn."

Ruby recovered completely over the fortnight at home. Anna and Paskal were thrilled to have her back, but now real life was calling her back. Now she had to fly away again, and spread her wings wide open.

A new chapter opened for Ruby after the PR startup she was working for got approved for an accelerator program in Holland.

Little did she know that Amsterdam is the new Paris!

"Look at this beauty!" Amsterdam was stunning, even in February. Ruby felt very fortunate to be living there, exploring a new land and meeting new people.

"Ruby, we need to go! We have to introduce ourselves to the rest of the 10 start-ups!" Katie called out

Katie was a colleague at work, she was usually the overseer of Ruby's work. She had long blonde hair and a kind, pink-lipsticked smile that said she was always there to help.

"I'm almost done with my hair, I'll be there any minute! Are we taking the bikes?" shouted Ruby

"Yes, I am already on it! Come on we are late!"

After an enjoyable, wintery ride they arrived safe and sound. It was the beginning of a new chapter, not only for work; but also for Ruby's private life. The day was full of meetings; making new relationships with new companies. Katie organised a party for the next evening at their place.

"Welcome, everyone! It is our honor to host this party tonight, so let's drink up and socialise. We have pizzas coming up soon and a lot more beer so get going!" yelled Ruby

Everyone was enjoying the party. As the night was just starting, someone in the crowd proposed that they move the party to the nearest coffee shop. Ruby wasn't to know then what lay in store for her at the after party.

There were so many of them that they had to occupy the biggest table in the coffee shop.

"Ruby, do you want to share a hash cake with me? I don't want to eat it alone" Katie asked

"It is my first time trying anything like this, but yes I would!" Ruby replied

After half an hour, all ten start-ups had had some of the cake and their laughter almost got them kicked out of the coffee shop. What happened next was life changing.

"Guys, would you like me to get some hash for all of us to smoke?" Asif asked the crowd 'Forget it, I'll just go and get some, why even bother asking! I know they'll want to try it anyway' he said to himself

After 5 minutes Asif came back to the table, but not alone.

"Hey, everyone I would like to introduce you to my best friend, Rashid. He just recommended me the best weed in town"

A year ago I was going through a lot. I started smoking weed again, and became more and more and burned out. During this time, I would go to coffee shops nowhere near my home. That particular day I decided to go to Katsu. When I entered I noticed a big group of people sitting on this table at the entrance. There was a Turkish guy at the door who asked me for a tip- what was my favourite weed? I told him and he invited me to sit on their big table as well. I was particularly placed between Ruby and Katie. Katie seemed not interested and left, so for me everyone was new and I was not focused on any one particularly.

"Best friend? When did you guys meet?" Ruby asked Asif

"Just now! He seems like a nice guy, so I invited him to join us, why not?!" Asif said

Rashid was very shy. He seemed nervous to join us; he didn't know what the situation was within the group; who was a couple and who was friendly with who, so he tried to be neutral. He picked a seat close to Ruby. After a while Katie decided to go home as she was not feeling well, which left Rashid and Ruby even closer together.

"How about we play some cards? Anyone?" suggested Rashid

"Yes, I'd love to teach you all to play a very funny Bulgarian game, called 'Bonjour Madame' which sounds French, I know!" Ruby replied

While they were playing cards Ruby felt a strong attraction build between her and Rashid; like a magnetic pull. She had never felt like this before. It was as if the whole world had stopped and all that mattered at that moment was the two of them. The rest of the group were just abstract objects, rarely there in the picture.

If you'd looked at Ruby's face that evening you would have seen pure sunshine; even her eyes were smiling from the energy between them. Slowly but surely, she was falling for Rashid. He, on the other hand, was very laid back and didn't seem to pay much attention to the energy between them. As they had just met, he didn't know if Ruby was even single. The night passed with lots of laughter and games and at the end Ruby wanted to take Rashid's number but didn't have the courage to ask. When time came to say goodbye Ruby was tormented by what action to take. She decided to play it smartly; she noticed that Rashid had given his number to one of her colleagues already so decided she'd ask him the next day instead of asking Rashid.

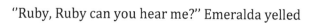

"Ruby, Ruby can you hear me?" Emeralda yelled

"Emeralda is that you? Am I dreaming?" Ruby asked

"Ruby, we are on the astral plane! I thought, as you are in the very high vibrational state of falling in love, it would be a good time to start your training to become an earth warrior. Tonight, we start with you learning more about active listening!" said Emeralda

"Emeralda, I do think I am in love, you're right! When Rashid sat next to me, I felt that energetic pull. It was as if his energy penetrated the core of my being. I stared into his eyes for a moment and a deep feeling of knowingness flooded my whole being. My eyes sparkled and my soul felt this wonderful, familiar connection. The way he speaks, the way he laughs; it was so resonant to me, despite the fact that on the surface we looked like two strangers, playing cards. Do you know this feeling?" Ruby asked

"As your higher self all I can tell you is that this is definitely not the first time your souls have met!" Emeralda replied

"Oh, what a relief! I thought I was going crazy." said Ruby

"Before we start with active listening, could you please tell me more about the name, Emeralda, means? I'm curious to know more about it."

"Our energy is very important Ruby. I hold the energy of the Emerald crystal." Emeralda began "It brings loyalty and provides for domestic bliss; it enhances unconditional love, unity and promotes friendship; it keeps partnerships in balance and can signal unfaithfulness if it changes colour. Emerald stimulates the heart chakra; having a healing effect on the emotions, as well as the physical heart. So, as you can see, our work is very much about connecting the mind to the heart and also; unconditional love. This is something we will dive into later on! Now I want you to sit cross legged, I will cover your eyes so you can focus your attention on everything else outside the visible world. Focus on the wind; how it feels on your skin, the birds singing in the distance, feel the earth (that gives you stability and foundation) beneath your feet."

"Alright, I will try to focus, but give me some time to practise this teaching. I will need time to master it" Ruby said, beginning to tune in "I am a tiger in a forest, I can feel how a tiger would feel the earth beneath its paws and feel the wind that gives it speed. I can see how my prey's pulse elevates when it sees my face. It's incredible. I have never sat in silence for a long time and focused on the details of the environment!"

Ruby was excited.

"I want you to practise this every night when you go to bed, and then implement it in your working life; this will increase productivity at work, and you will get better results. This is just the beginning of your training. In a month's time we will learn how you can channel healing power from your hands, so you can heal everything around you, even animals." Emeralda explained

"Thank you for being here for me Emeralda, and imparting such wisdom" Ruby said

"The knowledge is always inside you, as am I. Believe in yourself Ruby, and as I said before; you were always destined for big things in this life. This is just the first step on the road to success!"

Ruby kept practicing every night, as promised, and began implementing her new skills at work. Her productivity was rising, as was her salary. She was making the most sales and learning to actively listen to what the clients needed; offering solutions. She knew Emeralda was watching over her and when the time was right, she would visit her again.

—————◁◆▷—————

Hey Rashid, It was nice to meet you on Saturday playing

cards.

Hey bro! Yeah was nice meeting you guys.

It's Ruby by the way. But bro works too.

I thought you were the guy who sat next to me because I gave him my number? We played some crazy games. It was fun though. How are you doing?

Good I am glad you liked them. We are going to get together again this weekend if you'd like to join us again? I will give you the address soon!

Yes, I'd love to. Have a great day at work today!

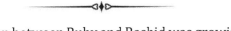

The connection between Ruby and Rashid was growing every day. They started talking for hours, getting to know each other, before the party that weekend.

The party was about to start. Ruby was still enjoying the Rijksmuseum with a few of her colleagues. Time was flying and she didn't even realise how late they all were for the party, and that Rashid was already there waiting for her!

Ruby took a taxi so she could reach Penelope's house faster. She was surprised to see the only person there was Rashid. He was dressed very well; with a tight T-shirt that showed off his great shape. Seeing every muscle perfectly formed underneath made Ruby imagine what it would feel like to explore his torso with her soft hands. His curly black hair was perfectly styled and then there was, of course, his smile, that swept Ruby off her feet.

Ruby was wearing a mustard dress, tights, and of course her signature red lipstick and green eyeshadow; with lots of mascara to underline her long eyelashes; making her hazel eyes pop. When both of them met again her heart stopped for a second. She couldn't think what to say; she was completely transfixed by his presence and lost her words.

Rashid accepted Ruby's apologies for her tardiness, saying he had had a nice chat with Penelope and then offered to help set up for the party.

Penelope was Ruby's best friend out of the new start-ups in Amsterdam. She was in her thirties, with long blonde hair, a fine figure and an Italian accent. She was also in sales, but in her heart still wanted to act. Penelope had had a bike accident that same day, she was too injured to set up the party, so Ruby and Rashid were in charge; which brought them closer together.

You could see in Rashid's face that he was happy to see Ruby again. While they set up, he played her a song called *Tedow* which Ruby thought sounded very romantic.

Ruby and Rashid got even closer during the party, the energy between them was rising. She was to be the catalyst; the spark that would allow the shy Rashid to express himself finally.

It was going well. All ten guests were drinking and playing cards, laughing as Ruby suggested playing 'Bonjour Madame' again. Later in the evening, she made Penelope lick Rashid's perfect abs in front of everyone; just to play the odds. She didn't want to let Rashid know how interested she was.

The night was coming to an end. Ruby asked Rashid if he was up for an after party at her place. The attraction had grown stronger as the evening had gone on and she could not hide it anymore. He seemed a bit hesitant.

"Do you want to go on an adventure?" she said

Rashid smiled in agreement. His cheeks flushed red, his heart beating fast in excitement. Rashid still couldn't quite process what was happening.

I put my eyes down to respect ladies bodies and not look at them with lust. That is something I was brought up with. It's about respect.

Ruby's energy was penetrating him to his core.

I did not expect it to happen so fast. I have been saving myself for more than six years. When Ruby invited me for an after party, I didn't know how to react.

When they arrived at her place, Ruby invited him to sit on the couch and lay down on his lap. They talked for an hour about topics ranging from biology and religion; to spirituality, dancing and yoga. Ruby tried to teach Rashid a bit more about alternative medicine and Human Design.

"Even though I can relate to some things that you have said or are into; there is a logical side of me that is critical. The reason that I have this side has to do with my breaking away from religious dogma in Islam. And probably also to do with being busy with science. It helped me break away from ideas that were harmful. I like evidence-based theories but at the same time, science can't explain everything (like the irrationality of our emotions etc.). Sometimes being somebody that is logical and critical protects you from ideas that are based on theories that cannot be proven. I like that, because some ideas are not always helpful and logic gives you the ability to see through lies that have no basis in logical thinking. On the other hand, it can be useful to believe in something- it can give you strength. It's kind of hard to only be logical and critical, because things have less meaning...if you know what I mean. So, for me, I am still trying to find a way to look at life from a perspective that isn't too logical but also not too irrational." Rashid said

Ruby realised he was more into science and logic than abstract thinking and faith, so she needed to let it go, instead deciding to ask him more about himself and his past.

"I was hurt so many times; conditioned by my family and religion. My father passed away when I was very young, my brother didn't really express his love for me, and I was always full of love, positivity and emotion." Rashid pouring his heart out

Ruby was on a mission to crack his heart open. She was intoxicated by his intellect, well-built body and sexy smile. Ruby sensed he was a very emotional being that had been through an awful lot in his life.

"I am originally from Morocco, but more precisely, a nomadic tribe that was once very fierce. I also had that fire burning inside me. But I was diagnosed with type 1 diabetes five years ago and my life has completely changed since then."

"Would you like to move this conversation into the bedroom? It's more comfortable." Ruby asked

Rashid did not even reply, he just followed her lead.

She is the lucky girl, after saving myself for six years now; this is it. Although I do feel that I am moving too fast, should I do it or not?

Lying on the bed only increased Ruby's appetite to taste his lips, she could not wait any more. She jumped on top of him, grabbing his curly black hair with one hand while with the other she started memorizing his sexy body, her lips making her way slowly from his neck slowly up to his cheek and then she looked at his eyes as she was waiting for that sexy look of his full of passion.

Their lips were the perfect match in size and softness. They started kissing with a passion that would have made the Gods jealous.

"Would you like to take a shower with me? Ruby said, stripping off her clothes

'Rashid was frozen for a moment. He had not been naked in front of a girl for so long. He was afraid Ruby would judge his appearance and the size of his cock. After a minute he decided to join Ruby in the shower, where they continued to explore each other's bodies with hands and kisses. Ruby made sure to comfort him; adoring every part of his body. Ruby loved feeling his skin next to hers. As the water rained down, making their bodies even more beautiful, Ruby went down on Rashid under the shower. He started moaning with pleasure as Ruby's tongue played with his head; stroking his shaft; she was merely teasing him before the real fun began. After the shower, Rashid lifted Ruby up and placed her on the bed. She laid, wrapped in a towel, her body still steaming hot. They were both so innocent. They spent some time eye-gazing before Ruby approached Rashid and kissed his lips gently. Rashid went down on Ruby.

He started from the top by kissing Ruby's cheeks slowly making his way to her lips, kissing softly. Ruby was full of excitement, you could see it; her body could not stop moving in Rashid's hands. He was making his way down her neck; first softly with his lips, then even softer with the tip of his tongue and then he started kissing and biting her so passionately that Ruby almost had an orgasm. He loved to tease her and play for a long time, just watching Ruby struggle, wanting his hard cock inside her. It gave him a lot of pleasure. He made his way to her breasts and started to gently press her nipples as Ruby moaned. He kissed them softly while making his way with his hand to her clit and started to give it a gentle rub. Ruby was pressing her hands on the pillow, grabbing the sheets with her fingers as Rashid continued the love-game for a while before he gave it to her completely. They made love for hours and Ruby was amazed that they both came very hard even though they just met. It was not just their lips that were perfectly matched in size and softness; their bodies were like missing parts of the puzzle, that fit together.

Ruby could not believe he hadn't had a girlfriend for the past 6 years, as his skills in bed were astonishing.

The next day Rashid stayed in bed while Ruby went to work. Surprisingly her energy was so high that she made a lot of sales that day. She trusted Rashid completely and even left him the keys for her house so he could rest. She was always so naive and trusting which was not always a good thing, but this time it worked well. Rashid decided to surprise Ruby with a meal so when she came home they had dinner together which made Ruby very happy. They learned a lot about each other every day. He stayed with her for 4 days after the party. Rashid's mother was worried, but he was having the time of his life.

On the second day, after work, they spent the night of doing things they both loved together like reading books, yoga and dancing. Ruby even challenged Rashid to a dance-off. The night was fun and ended up again in bed. They were two magnets that finally found each other, igniting the spark they needed to open their hearts. You could not tell from the outside that Rashid was anxious and stressed but he had his worries and Ruby was completely unaware.

On the third day Rashid had to go back to his house for a bit, to pick up some stuff he needed for his diabetes. He left Ruby with the following message:

There she stands, so representative as always
Ready to shake hands and make sales with no delays
Nothing will hold her back, you can see it in her eyes
Knows how to interact, she will catch you by surprise
Little do they know the struggles she goes through
The distance that she walks, from here to Timbuktu
The number of steps she'll take
Until her legs and feet will ache
A power nap is what she needs
After which she will proceed
Sleep and rest like you deserve
And charge up some of your reserves
You're doing great and you should know
And when you wake up ,please say 'Hello''!

Ruby woke with a big smile and went to work.

The days together were passing fast and before long it was time to say goodbye for the first time since they met, and it was hard on them both. Ruby was falling in love and it was quite obvious. Rashid went to the train station with Ruby to make sure she got on the right train to the airport and to say goodbye. They didn't know what lay in store for them.

"Goodbye, Rashid. I already miss you. I wish I could stay forever in your arms." Ruby whispered; tears falling down her face.

Rashid gave her one last hug and told her it was going to be ok and they would see each other soon. The flight from Amsterdam to London only took 45 minutes and the moment Ruby turned her phone back on, there were lots of messages from Rashid.

``There's no sunshine when she's gone" one said.

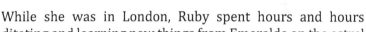

While she was in London, Ruby spent hours and hours meditating and learning new things from Emeralda on the astral plane.

"Ruby are you ready for the big day?" Emeralda asked "Today I will be teaching you how to use the crystal tattoo you have; on your forehead; and how to use the selenite wand to crystallize and de-crystallize on Sirius B. Then we will be done meeting here on the astral plane. It's time for you to see the Castle! Are you ready?"

"I was born ready!" Ruby replied

"Ok, take your wand and put it on your forehead over the Om symbol, I want you to command the wand with your mind to decrystallize your body from the Earth and direct your energy and attention to Sirius B where it will crystalize (appear). Together, on the count of three- 1....2...3...."

Ruby got her position and wand ready. From the outside she looked very focused on what she was doing, but while Emeralda disappeared immediately; Ruby didn't. Ruby's first attempt was not successful!

"I see Ruby did not make it back with you my child" Celeste noticed

"Let's give her some time. I am sure she will appear!" Emeralda smiled to cover her nervousness

"Come on- focus Ruby, you can't be scared; you are a warrior." Emeralda willed "One, two, three."

Ruby managed to decrystallize as the wand projected its powerful energy outwards, touching her skin. Her whole body started dissolving into crystal dust from head to toe!

Sirius B

Buzz buzz buzz- the sound of crystallization pierced the air.

Emeralda and Celeste stared eagerly at the crystals starting to form Ruby's body.

Ruby's crystallization on Sirius B was finally complete!

"Welcome home my child" said Celeste with a proud smile "You finally made it! I will show you around another time because today is dedicated to your next lesson!"

"Thank you mother, Emeralda is a great teacher!"

"Ruby, today's lesson will be about how to expand the energy of your heart beyond yourself." Celeste began "Before we start, I would like to mention something I have been waiting to announce: From the moment you step into the Crystal Palace, your blood is no longer red like before; it is now a crystal liquid; which means you no longer require earth's food to sustain you. You can recharge in the sun. You need to know that the heart's energy is the purest form; that is why emotions are so powerful. Emotion means energy put into motion. Now, close your eyes and focus on your heartbeat. Feel it, like you are in the chambers of your heart. Now I want you to imagine that your heart is a crystal and inside that heart, there is a hidden jewel. What does the jewel looks like Ruby?"

"It looks purple, dark purple!" Ruby replied

"Good. Continue to focus on it, and the light that it shines. Now, draw that light from your heart up to the throat and then up to the forehead; feel the light pulsing in your third eye; then fill the crown chakra with it. As you feel your whole-body vibrating, shoot the light up to the sky and also back down to earth. Now expand the light, seeing it expand from the front and back of the body. Keep expanding; hold the frequency from the heart; feel it expanding in all directions and hold. In your mind hold that same vision, whilst you try to increase the intensity of the heart vibration."

Ruby kept practicing all night while everyone on Earth was sleeping safe and sound; she knew that one day this skill would be needed, but she didn't know how soon.

The next morning Ruby woke up with a mild headache. She exchanged a few messages with Rashid and then received another poem from him:

Her body is beautiful like a painting of Van Gogh
How she dances and get low
She really knows how to put on a show
Loves and hates it when I go slow

Until she reaches that plateau
And rides those waves that go up and below
She only has a few days to go
After that she can get out of this flow
And get massaged like dough
By that guy with the afro

"Oh my God Rashid! I feel very flattered; you never really talk about your feelings, especially when it comes to my body!" said a beaming Ruby. "How are you feeling today?" she asked

Rashid didn't really feel like talking that day so he shared another poem with Ruby instead.

Hypoglycemia

It brings me down and low
It gets my body out of its flow
It wakes me up in a panic state
Please hypo not now, it's late
Sometimes it comes when I'm awake
Sometimes it hits like an earthquake
Unannounced it knocks on my door
Oh there it is, the hypo once more

The craving for sweets is oh so strong
The hypo also takes it's friends along
Sadness, sweaty palms and blurry eyes
Makes me miss those sugar highs
I need to treat myself now quick
If I don't I might fall like a brick
The aftermath stays after the hypo is gone
The tightness in my muscles, it feels like stone

It feels like dying all over again
I need to breathe and count to ten
This feeling will pass and go away
I hope this gets better someday

I want to work and live my life
But I stay at home like a housewife
Impaired and beaten I sometimes feel
I need some yoga and time to heal.

Ruby felt bad that Rashid's health worsened while she was away.

"Baby, can I come and see you soon?" Ruby asked on the phone that evening "Maybe come and stay with you at your place?"

"Ruby, I live with my mum and I have to be honest, she will probably never allow me to bring you home with me. You are Christian; I need to get my own place to be able to host you" Rashid said "But I can always rent a place for us? We could go on a road trip if you want? We'll do something soon."

Ruby's eyes welled with tears. His words felt like swords in her heart. She felt unworthy and unwanted. She tried to smile through the pain.

"Yes, I'd love that. I could come in a couple of weeks' time and we could go for a road trip to the beach!" she said

"Sure, I'll call the pineapple express line right away
Makes it taste better for feast day

And I'll go down on you anyway you please
I might even give you a strip tease
Won't stop until you will yell please!
I'll tell you to go through the unease of the tease;

I will make a reservation right away!" Rashid said

Ruby could not contain her laugh as the poem was too funny. She bought her ticket to Amsterdam right away and was excited to go to work; the thought of Rashid and being in his arms was keeping her positive, and she was learning so much on Sirius B. It was a profound transformation for Ruby. But although she was working in London, her heart was in Amsterdam.

Two weeks later Ruby arrived at Schiphol Airport and Rashid was there to pick her up.

"I am so happy to see you. Finally in your arms." Ruby said and hugged Rashid tight, kissing him

"I am so happy to see you back here Ruby. It seems so long since you were here. I have planned to visit the Parklandschap De Oeverlanden today; we can spend the whole day; I've got food, blankets and music. How is that as a plan for day one?" Rashid asked

"Wow, babe. You are well prepared! I can't wait. Let's go!"

Ruby was so excited to be back. There was a sparkle in her eyes when she saw him again, he made her heart beat faster and her smile smile wider.

They spent the whole day together, playing cards, listening to music, relaxing and enjoying each other's company.

"Tomorrow, my boss and his friends are organizing a boat party." Ruby said as they watched the sunset; which felt all the more special with him "We will be sailing on the canals, sipping some wine... would you like to join us?"

"Yes, I'd love to. You know, I've lived my whole life in Amsterdam and never been on a boat cruise on the canals! Thank you Ruby" Rashid said

They spent the following days having fun. Partying on the boat the next day was the first time Ruby had seen Rashid a bit tipsy; but she really liked how chilled he was with all her friends.

They kissed on the bow of the boat in the gentle sunset rays, while the others' partied.

It was as if the crowd and the sun were a mere background to the magic happening in Rashid and Ruby's hearts.

Rashid felt a bit uncomfortable at first; he wasn't a fan of kissing too much in public, but after a few drinks he loosened up.

"Baby, I need to tell you something. Tomorrow my boss is sending me to Paris to attend this huge event to try and close some deals with entrepreneurs. I will be back Saturday though so we can still go on our road trip like we said" Ruby whispered

"Wow you just arrived babe, I've barely had a chance to see you properly and now you are leaving me again for two days! You will have to make it up to me" said Rashid with a smile

"I will make sure of it! Let's now enjoy tonight." Ruby promised, and turned back to the party "Guys shall we stop the boat here? Listen! They are having a beach party over there. Let's park the boat and have some fun" Ruby screamed

The next morning Ruby left early with the rest of the start-ups to Paris. While she rested her body on the train; her mind was busy.

After months of seeing each other it was crystal clear to her. Ruby's gut feeling had been spot on. Ruby and Rashid were soulmates. He was her mirror; he reflected all her wounds and her good qualities back to her.

She spent two days at the event, trying to make contact with more than a hundred people, to bring more business to her PR company. At the end of her first day she called Rashid.

"Hello babe, guess where I am?" Ruby turned the camera on on her phone.

"Oh my god! The Eiffel Tower! Wow, it's beautiful. I wish I could join you there; everyone seems to be enjoying themselves with a picnic! Try to enjoy it as much as possible. Thank you for sharing this moment with me" he said.

Ruby's father called her about once a month to check on her:

"Hey Ruby. How's life treating you?"

"Well, I am in Paris at the moment, but back to Amsterdam soon. I'm staying there for a couple of months before going back to London. Actually, yes I do have news. I have a boyfriend. I met him on my second day in Amsterdam." Ruby smiled

"Oh wow that is exciting news. Is he Dutch?" he asked

"He's from Morocco but has been living in Holland since he was born. Why?" Ruby asked

"Ruby, you know I would never accept him for you if he is Moroccan; they have a different faith to us. I have seen so many of them here in Spain and I don't like how they treat women. You break up this relationship immediately, or you forget you have a father!"

"But dad, I love him. I can't just break up because you want me to. Remember my last relationship? He was Bulgarian and it was the worst relationship I've ever had. I got with him so you and mum would be happy, as he spoke Bulgarian, not because I was madly in love with him." Ruby explained

"This conversation is over, Ruby. This is for your own good, one day you'll understand."

Ruby hung up the phone and started crying. Just when everything between them had started to bloom and they were falling for each other. She felt hopeless once again, as the support of her parents diminished. She looked around at the couples enjoying champagne in the meadows in front of the tower and thought about how she could never have this with Rashid.

Ruby's phone buzzed.

> **She is a working bee**
> **Almost never free**
> **Multi-tasking everyday**
> **Doesn't even drink much coffee a day.**

He always knew how to cheer her up.

The next day Ruby arrived back in Amsterdam where Rashid was waiting to pick her up and start their road trip. Ruby tried to forget her father's words and put on a smile.

After about an hour's drive, Ruby woke up from snoozing. Everything was green and peaceful. The roads were so straight and empty. She felt relaxed.

"Are we close?" Ruby glanced over at Rashid

"Yes we're almost there, you woke up just in time!"

Ruby never imagined Holland had such a great beach. Ruby started running over the soft, smooth sand to the sea as Rashid unloaded the bags from the trunk. She had fallen in love with life again. She felt peaceful, balanced and recharged. And she knew that when she was with Rashid, nothing bad could happen. She always felt safe with him.

That afternoon Rashid bought out a surprise for Ruby.

"What is this, honey?" she said

"Magic mushrooms! Would you like to go on a deeper

spiritual trip with me? Welcome to Den Helder! I hope you like the beach." Rashid offered

"I've never tried them, but I'm willing to give it a go. How much do I have to take?" Ruby replied with excitement

Rashid explained to Ruby about the possible effects and downsides before they started exploring psychedelics.

"I will distribute them evenly. Here is your part. Let's start. We can eat later as it's better to do these on an empty stomach. Cheers! Let the trip begin'

Ruby had a surprise for Rashid too, and decided to share it with him.

"This poem is specially dedicated to the love of my life:
The one that holds a very special place in my heart
The one that knows me inside and out
The one that is always welcomed in my life

You came and changed my life for the better
You showed me love and care like no other
Exploring different dimensions and realities
And tuning each other's breaths and heart beats

You the special one I knew from the start
The first time I met you, your energy was imprinted onto me

When I look into your eyes tripping, I lose myself in the softness of your lips that make me feel I am melting into you and there is no way back but to follow your lead

You always know what to say and do to bring back my smile and light in my heart

*I see you for who you are even in your darkest days I know
the kind soul behind the tears*

*I love you with all my heart and soul
And sometimes I see your love is shining too*

*No matter the distance and any obstacles in our way
I will be there waiting for you to reach out
And when the time is right we will be together."*

"Thank you so much Ruby, it really means a lot!" Rashid said
with tears in his eyes

"I am starting to see things" Ruby said "The clouds are
moving in a very strange direction, I can even see the energy
surrounding the grass."

After a moment Ruby's pupils were black; the green
completely vanished!

"Oh my God! I am in Egypt! Oh wow, I've never been to Egypt
before. I can see the pyramids and Orion's belt. It feels like I am
on the balcony of a building and someone is trying to call my
name."

She turned around and was back on the beach with Rashid.
Ruby closed her eyes and tried to focus on the sensation of the
mushrooms.

"Here we go again! I see Isis, the goddess of magic, fertility
and motherhood, and death, healing and rebirth. She is calling
my name...

"Ruby, Ruby, find the ruby. Return to Egypt..."

The voices started to fade away. Her trip was almost over; the
drugs were fading. Ruby was trying to make sense of what she
just saw.

"Babe are you alright?" Rashid touched her shoulder "You seemed to get carried away. Did you enjoy your first trip? We have been on the beach for 3 hours! You should see your face! It's lobster red! You forgot to put sunscreen didn't you?"

"I had the most profound experience, Rashid. I think I saw Isis in Egypt. I have never travelled to Egypt. Cheaper than flying!" Ruby laughed. "Yes it was a great experience, thank you! I can feel my face on fire though. We should go back to Airbnb and get some rest."

On the way back to the car, Ruby saw these huge sand dunes and all she could think was that she wanted to lie between them

"Can we? Just for a moment?" Ruby screamed
"Yes, of course. I'll wait for you. Off you go." Rashid said

"Oh my God! I feel one with the sand! Actually, I think I *am* sand."

She made sand angels moving her legs and arms. It felt so relaxing. She was soothed to be one with the sand.

Before bed that night, Ruby decided to connect with Emeralda, as the vivid trip she had was still without answers.

"Emeralda, are you here? I need to ask you something very important!" Ruby called

"Yes, Ruby I am here. How can I help with your spiritual journey?"

"I had a vision of Isis. She was telling me to find Ruby? I didn't get what that was about. Was she calling my name or did she want me to find a crystal?" Ruby asked

"Ruby, in your past you were buried in the Pyramids of Egypt.

This is a past life vision you were having; but the message seems to be from the present. I could help you to go back to your past life and find out what you need to do?" Emeralda suggested

"Let's do it. I'm ready! I am sure Rashid won't notice; he is deeply asleep. I just don't know how long, as his blood sugar wakes him up at night a lot.

"Hurry then" said Emeralda "Let's go to the healing room. I have my black spot quartz there. It helps with reading akashic records. It will help you to get back to your past life!"

Emeralda showed Ruby part of her house; Ruby was completely amazed. Everything was made of different crystals; even the beds were of crystal.

"Do you sleep here on Sirius B? I see you have beds but they don't look like our beds at all?" Ruby asked

"We charge ourselves by laying on the crystal beds for a bit; we don't need to sleep as you do. Our bodies are a bit different in terms of operation and what is needed to live. We have different crystal beds for different occasions. This one, for example, helps us to forget painful memories and heal. The other one on your left, balances the energies in the body." Emeralda explained. "Lie down and close your eyes. I will close the bed; it needs to be closed like a shell to activate. Now, think about what you saw on the beach and the crystal will help you download more information from that exact past life. Understood?"

"Understood" said Ruby

The moment Ruby closed her eyes the vision started to unfold:

"Isis is again in front of me. She looks so beautiful. I see she wants me to follow her; so I do. She brings me to the Pyramid."

"Ruby, I knew you would come back. Do you remember this pyramid? We used to spend a lot of time here together. Now it's your time, in this lifetime, to save the world. Take this ruby crystal as a gift from me; when time is right you will know what to do! Now you must go, the clock is ticking." Isis whispered

Ruby didn't have a chance to speak; she was trying to process all this information and piece the puzzle together. Ruby opened the shell and noticed the crystal was already in her hands.

"My God! I have it here in my hands." Ruby was overwhelmed and dizzy.

"Ruby, relax; mother Isis is the protector Goddess on Sirius A. She is a fellow Sirian- even though they are way more serious than us" Emeralda laughed. "We like to party more and our climate is different. One day we can teleport to Sirius A. I am pretty sure you won't like the cold though. Let me tell you a bit about them. They do shadow work; they like the dark arts; they can scan you and read you like a book, and can sometimes be a bit unapproachable. What we have in common is that we are following our mission in life; helping to remove injustice on the lower planes. Contrary to their scene; we have all the fun and parties, and all the crystals you can imagine. On Sirius B we are more welcoming, positive beings. Sometimes way too positive."

Emeralda advised that Ruby get some rest; so she did. Emeralda put her wand onto Ruby's tattoo and Ruby descended to her bed on Earth with the ruby crystal on her nightstand.

CHAPTER FIVE

Lightning Strikes

The next day they left Den Helder to visit Texel, an island outside the Netherlands. When Ruby woke up, Rashid was not next to her instead there was a piece of paper with a poem on it.

This poem I'm writing just for you.

The one that likes to write to me too
The one that heals with her hands
The one that likes to stick to the plans
The one that listens and understands
The one that likes to lay in the sands

Her fire is burning hot and bright
She will not stand back for the fight
Far from home she chose to stand
And make her way throughout the land
She's always flying from place to place
We barely see each other face to face

But now we've made that rendezvous
She might get stuck to me like glue
She likes to explore, venture too

The trip is amazing, I like it too
When she's in panic and restless inside
I say the right words to calm back her mind

Just as she wakes up and looks at her phone
And wipes her eyes to see that beautiful poem
He Hopes that she likes it, and brings her a smile
It's not complicated, it's my artistic style
The last thing I'll say is good night to you
This poem is too long, don't want to overdo.

" Come and join me for breakfast downstairs, beautiful!"
Rashid called out

Ruby smiled; her heart bathed in this loving energy. She was told to go downstairs; so she did.

Rashid had planned the whole journey very well. After breakfast, they had to catch a boat to get to Texel and then they rented bikes to go around; the island was perfect for biking.

"Babe it is just so peaceful here. I feel like we are in the infinite valleys! And it's amazing you can bike next to the coast line; seeing the beach, and smelling the ocean. It is the greatest surprise, very good choice!" Ruby was ecstatic

They spent the whole day lying on the beach, playing cards, listening to music and of course, dancing! As the sun set, Ruby focused her gaze deeply on the horizon.

"I love to see the reflection of the sunset rays on your face." said Rashid "Your eyes are so beautiful and your charming smile! You're an angel!"

Ruby smiled broadly and looked straight into Rashid's eyes. She stood up and walked very slowly to Rashid who was smoking his cigarette. His eyes were just following her movement and nothing else; his focus was entirely on Ruby's figure.

"I love you Rashid!" Ruby whispered with a smile on her face and that sparkle he gave her in her eyes "I have loved you since the first day I met you! You are very special to me!"

Rashid was silent. He smiled and only nodded in agreement.

The day was almost gone, so they headed back to Airbnb. They were staying with an amazing couple in a very posh neighborhood. The women who owned the place had a huge tent in her garden where she was teaching yoga and meditation. Ruby was astonished to see it as she was herself, very interested in spirituality. The owners invited Rashid and Ruby for dinner so they could get to know one another. It turned out that they had tried Ayahuasca; the secret plant medicine from the Amazon, that helps you with spiritual ascension.

They spoke a lot about their spiritual journey as the night went on, while Ruby and Rashid listened carefully. They wanted to try that plant someday too.

Ruby and Rashid's love life was getting better and better; every single time their bodies touched each other. What they thought in the beginning was the best experience now paled in comparison to what they had now. After 4 amazing days of exploring new places in Holland; the pancake house, animals in the forest, Texel island's nice bars and restaurants on the beach, and a vast valley of perfect scenery to enjoy biking; it was time for Ruby to go back to London. The sadness was overwhelming.

"You should come visit me sometime Rashid. I would love to show you around!" Ruby said
"It would be my pleasure" he replied " I have never been to London! I will see what I can do- as you know I am flying to Morocco next week to be with my family for three weeks!"

They hugged each other very tightly; the impending absence

filling their hearts as Ruby left Rashid's arms. The one and only place she always felt safe was always so far away. She felt like a child has been taken from its mother at birth; their attachment to each other was huge. The waves went very high when they spent time together, but very low when they were apart-the difference was almost unbearable! An addict would say it was like a drug withdrawal; leaving you lonely and depressed.

It was 17 of June, 2019 when Rashid went on his family vacation to Marrakech. Of course, Ruby was still in London waiting for his calls. She was addicted to his love.

Ruby's phone buzzed across the table

"Hello Ruby, how are you doing?" Rashid asked, in a detached tone of voice

"I'm well, babe, just about to cook some food. How are you? How's Morocco? I bet it's nice and the sun is shining, not raining like in London!" Ruby said with a smile.

"Ruby" Rashid paused. "I've been thinking a lot and I think it is best for us to split up. We have so many differences; it will be impossible to be together. On the one hand I want to be with you because you are nice. On the other hand, I have so much on my plate already. I am dealing with depression and diabetes; I have no room in my life for this. I am sorry. I guess I can't live up to the expectations you have. I think it is best to stop talking to each other completely, so we can forget and move on."

In that moment Ruby's heart broke into pieces again; the heart that was just beginning to heal after her grandmother's death. Ruby didn't even have the strength to respond; she just hung up the phone. That triggered the abandonment feeling in her heart!

Her breath was short. She felt like a wounded deer laying in the forest, breathing slowly while the blood dripped from the wound, waiting for a slow and painful death. A million thoughts ran through her head as she tried to explain this to herself. She decided to put all this pain away and write a poem to deal with her heart break:

Lightning

Have you ever been in love?

Well, I have. Let me tell you how it feels!

Time stops when we're together nothing else matters, but him.

Hours together seemed like just a moment, I noticed every detail, his eyelashes trembling from the sunlight on the beach.

Honesty, openness, no judgement, just us.

Hugging together, no need for words, just silence and two hearts beating simultaneously, priceless. We both shine our heavenly light on to grow and expand. To fight fear, anxiety negative talks from the outside world, we break the mask. We touch gently exploring our perfectly matching bodies, the sensation of my fingertips feeling his soft mocha skin, makes my whole-body tremble wanting more. Our lips perfectly matched together - the size, the softness, the kiss in which we lost each other as we are both one-no separation. Our conversations are always deep, touching every sense and emotion. I believe he is my soulmate as we make love we intertwine in other dimensions. We are devoted to each other and giving full satisfaction to the other with a heart full of passion.

Passion to give, passion to eat the other like a hungry animal. This desire I see in his dark brown chocolate eyes, mocha skin, sexy body that drives every single cell in my body to Heaven. My hands melting in his curly black hair, leaving me breathless. At that moment the chemistry goes off the roof, his magic touch and kisses when we make love make me want to know more, to experience more. When I bite my lip, gazing at his eyes, he knows this moment I'm ready for the kiss. Kiss not like any other, I can feel the taste, the sweetness, then the lightning strikes:

Back to reality, I sense the separation winning:

Religions, two unhappy parents- I couldn't care less ...but here we go the lightning strikes again:

He brings me back to reality when he says: I want to let you go!

And he did let me go. He said fear is bigger than the love we share. I feel powerless, I feel so small, I feel lost.

Then I realise how much power the outside world has over us, I realise I have to stay strong, grounded, true to myself to be able to continue to love.

In your arms, you hold me tight
I thought you will never let me go through the night.
All my dreams were peaceful because of you
Holding me in your arms like you do.
Today my heart is aching for a man
that is far away and I have to understand
No matter what I do
He is ready to let go.
Sexy body and a charming smile
are now somewhere in a mile away.
Dark black curly hair and a deep chocolate eyes
Magic touch and a nice vibe.
What should I do?
When I am still in love with you?
You walked away, I have no choice.
You broke my heart, you tore me apart.
Every moment I wait for you,
Lying to myself our love was true.

Your absence makes more tears flow.
That is when I know,
I have to let go.

Rashid stopped texting Ruby to see if he could live without her. For him, the distance was too much to bear and then of course, there was his family. He was used to running away or using drugs to deal with negative emotions instead of dealing with them.

Ruby didn't want to eat at all, she laid in bed like a wounded animal waiting to die. All she could think about were all the wonderful memories of them together and the moments of pure love and happiness. These memories stabbed like a sharp knife in her kind heart, even bleeding love; she was still deeply in love with Rashid.

After two weeks of silence; after causing the heartbreak that left Ruby with no energy to eat or do her daily tasks; Ruby felt so much pain. She was living in a country by herself surrounded with all these people, but still feeling empty in her heart. All she wanted to do is talk to the one and only person that could help her pain-her grandma.

"I am reaching out to you for advice, knowing you will never answer." Ruby said to herself as she meditated

"I am here Ruby" came a voice "Come and join me in this magical place - you will always find me here; in the hidden cave with the private beach and crystal-clear water; where the dolphins are ever present. I heard your prayers and I came to tell you that your heart is stronger than you think and that I have the feeling this is not the end between you and Rashid. Be strong and calm; wait for the storm to pass; the sun will rise again. But be aware that there is more to Rashid than meets the eye." Radka advised her granddaughter.

"Thank you grandma - you always know exactly what to say to calm me down. I love this place! It looks like heaven. Is that where you live now?" Ruby started to smile again

"Yes, Ruby. This is where my soul is healing before I go on to another soul journey to Earth." Radka said

"Grandma, can you reincarnate as my child or something? I would love to have you back into the family." Ruby asked

"I am not sure yet, Ruby, if I can give such an answer; but I will think about it! But now is the time for you to heal. I know one of your dreams has been to swim with dolphins - here you have the chance to do so and heal your wound. Go for it!

Get in the healing waters, they already know what to do with you."

Ruby could not swim at all, but she jumped in without hesitation completely trusting her grandma. Ruby spent some time bathing in the healing waters, swimming with the dolphins and making connections with them. Little did she know that her connection to dolphins and their healing powers was to continue.

Finally, after weeks of silence, Rashid started to communicate again.

⊲◆⊳

Sirius B

"Ruby, today I will be teaching you why and how to use a crystal singing bowl. First here are some of the benefits and how to do it!" Celeste explained

Crystal singing bowls are used with yoga, sound healing, crystal cleansing, space clearing and to signify the beginning and end of meditation. Running the mallet around the bowl with slight

pressure will create the tone. When this happens, the bowl is said to sing, hence its name. They create a range of sounds to restore the normal vibratory frequencies of diseased and out-of-harmony parts of the body, mind and soul.

There are many benefits to using crystal singing bowls, here are just a few:

1). Significantly reduces stress and anxiety
2). Stimulates the immune system
3). It assists with lowering blood pressure and anger
4). Deep relaxation and pain relief
5). Assists with chakra cleansing and balancing
6). Helps to calm overactive adrenals
7). Increases mental and emotional clarity

The notes of the crystal singing bowls correspond with each of the major chakras. Chakras can be described as energy centres of the body. Each energy centre has unique aspects and corresponds with specific tones of the musical scale. Keeping these centres in balance results in health and harmony.

The chakras are very well symbolized on Earth with the Christmas tree, the awakening of the Kundalini energy!

At the base of your spine is the 1st Root chakra, it is connected to the Earth element, colour red, the right to have and issues connected to the physical needs. Moving up to the lower abdominal is the 2nd Sacral chakra, it is connected to the Water element, the colour orange, to feel your emotions and sexuality. Solar plexus is the 3rd yellow chakra, it is connected to the fire element and your will power, to act. Moving up is the 4th Heart Chakra, located in the heart, corresponding to love and Air element. The colour of the chakra is green. The throat is the 5th chakra corresponding with the Sound element. The ability to communicate and speak the truth, the colour is blue. The Third eye is the 6th chakra located in the Brow, corresponds to the element of Light and the ability to see intuitively. The colour is indigo for this chakra. The last of the main 7 chakras is the Crown chakra, located at the top of your head like a lotus. The element is Though and the ability to know and understand on a cosmic level. The colour is violet.

"Now, I am going to play the bowl, and I want you to lie down and just feel the sound. You will feel the resonance with one of your chakras. I will teach you to focus and feel the frequency of each chakra, so let's begin."

Celeste and Ruby were in the healing room doing crystal singing bowls for hours. Celeste would strike the bowl and start the flow around Ruby's body, activating the so-called junk DNA and removing blockages. Now she had finally learned how to travel to Sirius B with her physical body, she could learn more things that would help humanity than when she could only do astral travel. Spending all this time with Celeste really boosted her healing capabilities; she was getting to know her true nature, as well as her mother.

Ruby was transforming bit by bit; every time visiting Sirius B and she was bringing all this knowledge to planet Earth.

"Great lesson Ruby!" said Celeste

"Next time I will teach you how to resonate with animals and even make them bow to your will; so they can assist you on Earth; instead of you being afraid of them"

"Thank you, mother, I can't wait for my next lesson!" said Ruby excitedly

"Patience my child, everything comes in time. Patience and persistence are key to growing and developing. You also need to be patient with Rashid; sometimes you rush- not everyone on Earth develops with the speed of light like you do. You need to be mindful of that and give him time. See you tomorrow same time" Celeste explained

"I will, mother. Thank you for all the knowledge and loving energy!" Ruby put the selenatine wand on her forehead and crystalized herself back to Earth!

CHAPTER SIX

The Crystal Palace

The Crystal Palace had an underwater world; where all the mermaids and mermen lived; where pearls were forming.

On the surface everything was covered in crystals and tall transparent buildings. The sun was shining high when they arrived and the Castle was full of different Sirian species; from the mermaids with long red or blond hair and hazel eyes to suit their skin tone and tail; to blue sirians; to crystal citizens with shiny skin and no hair; and finally the mermen- tall and handsome with great manes and well-built bodies. There were crystal cats flying around serving drinks, but not the typical cocktails you'd expect; healing waters for longevity! The party for Ruby's homecoming was in full swing. Everyone had prepared a welcome gift from ferry pearls to different crystal earrings, bracelets, and even crystal outfits!

Ruby had finally perfected how to use her selenite to crystallize and de-crystallize her earthly body to Sirius B, where her mother Celeste was waiting to show her around.

"Wonderful skills, Ruby! Welcome to your home coming party!" Celeste said and then turned to address the crowd

"Everyone, may I have your attention please! I would like to formally introduce you to Ruby, she made it home! Cheers everyone and let the party begin!"

Ruby was looking very afraid and nervous. Everyone was waving and looked so happy to see her, but there was one problem; she couldn't understand why they didn't speak!

"Mother, thank you for the big introduction; but why is no one speaking?" Ruby asked

Ruby could understand only Celeste as they were genetically connected.

"My apologies honey, do you not understand our light language?" Celeste turned to Emeralda

"I must have forgotten to teach her that" said Emeralda guiltily

Celeste addressed the crowd again:

"My dear Crystal citizens, fellow Sirians, would you be so kind as to welcome Ruby and speak the earth language for today, as she has not yet learned the light language of Sirius B!"

All of a sudden Ruby was overwhelmed with greetings, as all the Sirians, mermaids and mermen at the party started speaking her language!

"Mother, this place is unbelievable." she said "I am in love and so happy to be here! I did not imagine it to look like this! It's beyond my imagination! And the underwater world was a huge surprise! Oh! Are all these presents for me?"

"Of course, my child; these gifts are a sign of our appreciation for your efforts in the Sirian world!" Celeste replied

Emeralda looked very similar to her mother, but her robe was of course green; and her Princess crown was made of perfectly polished Emerald crystals. Her eyes were also green- not blue like Celeste's. Her skin and body structure was the same though; tall, silver-like shiny skin and a very fine figure. Celeste's throne was positioned right in the middle of the room with a perfect view to every corner of the dancefloor.

"Now" said Celeste "Allow me to show you the Fountain of Life; its crystalline, healing water helps you to stay young and vibrant. One sip is enough to recharge every cell of your body so you start dancing in perfect harmony. The majestic lotus is hidden under the water; it only shows when you need some extra healing and it has a hidden jewel inside that can help you deal with any disharmony you may have. The jewel can be anything from a diamond to a ruby or emerald- depending on your needs. Would you like to try, Ruby?" Celeste asked

Ruby nodded in agreement. As she got closer to the fountain; to grab the crystal cup with healing waters; the golden lotus emerged from the depths. It was so bright, it looked like golden energy in the form of a lotus, then it opened its petals and revealed an emerald jewel.

"Take it, Ruby. It is yours!" said Celeste

Ruby extended her fingertips and gently approached the jewel whilst trying not to hurt the lotus. As she was saying 'Thank you' the lotus folded its petals and disappeared again. Ruby was still feeling confused as to why the lotus would give her an Emerald as a gift of healing; but she knew deep down that time would show her when to use it!

"So, do you have schools as we have on Earth?" Ruby asked Celeste

"No Ruby, we are still evolving and aim to get to the 7th Dimension process; but we do not have schools as you would think of them. But I will show you what we do have in the Crystal Palace."

Celeste wanted to show Ruby the Palace so she could feel at home, just like Emeralda.

"Ruby, I want you to understand that our core value here is unity; helping each other on the path of ascension. We know we are not separate from each other, and, in order to make it work we need everyone putting in the work. There is no division. In the sixth dimension, as you can see, there is still a female and a male energy; but the higher you go in evolution, this dissolves too."

Celeste brought Ruby to a very tall, transparent building that looked like a giant glasshouse- but it was made of crystal-clear quartz. It was very warm inside, as the sun's rays penetrated the crystal, allowing the bright sunlight to warm the whole space. There were no chairs and tables, and no books as you would see in a real school on Earth- there was only one crystal in the middle of the room, on top of which an energy ball floated in the air; sending beams of light upwards.

"What is that ball of energy?" asked a curious Ruby

"We are the Knowledge Keepers" Celeste explained "We have access to the Akashic Records; our Library of Light. The energy makes its way down from the ball into this Amethyst crystal that we can touch and have access to anything that has happened, is about to happen, and the different possibilities of what could happen in the future"

"It sounds a bit like 'Google' on Earth - but much cooler than that!" Ruby smiled

As Ruby and Celeste were walking they saw a falling star.

"If you could use a wish right now Ruby, what would you like to manifest? Let's practice some manifestation- it is vital for your personal development! Anything that comes to mind?" Celeste asked

"I imagine a building in the heart of London, made of self-sustainable materials. We have all the alternative practices in the world under one roof, and teaching beyond our world. From financial freedom, to self-help for spiritual development. It's a tall building, mostly made of glass, warm- with lots of sunlight. And a lovely garden with organic plants. I see it as a three story building combining all human needs: Body, Mind and Spirit. " Ruby explained gesticulating wildly

"Very well my child! I like the idea a lot. What else do you see in this visualization?" Celeste urged Ruby to continue

"I imagine a big, black onyx fountain in the middle of the first floor that will absorb all the negative energy and prevent the students from feeling drained. A reception and a library on the first floor, as well as a kitchen where lessons can be taught on how to use plants as medicine. Practices like Ayurveda and mindful organic eating can be offered, to aid a healthy lifestyle. The second floor would be all about the creative arts- music, painting, singing. It's so intoxicating. Oh! I picked up a vision of the third floor being all about healing practices such as reiki, crystal healing, animal healing, human design, as well as manifestation and visualization."

"Well done Ruby; everything is energy before it becomes matter." said Celeste "Use your creative force for the greater good! I am very proud of your first manifestation. As an advanced soul, and my daughter, you always see the bigger picture by moving the focus on the collective. Now, you must always give names to your creations, so what would the name be?"

"The Universal Wisdom Institute" said Ruby, closing her eyes to imagine all the people and circumstances she would need to turn this project into a reality on Earth.

"Now, I will leave you with Emeralda- she will teach you our language. I'm going to the party!" Celeste laughed.

"Light language is a form of communication that bypasses human limitations around the meaning of words. It provokes a shift to a higher frequency and puts you in a Gamma state. Light is sound, Ruby, and sound- is vibration. So, remember that our language is based on vibration. For example, I will give you the sound of a bird singing: It is a type of vibrational frequency that you perceive as a song on the earth plane; but in reality, it is a language that your brain is not able to decode. On Sirius B, we speak telepathically; which means that my thoughts manifest as a wave of vibration that is sent to you by my intention. Our brains then perceive this wave as information, and decode it. Then, you send me a wave back- without even opening your mouth! Here, everything is vibration; our bodies, our language and even our names carry the specific vibrations of crystals. So, let's try it! I will send you my thoughts and you will try to feel them in your brain and send a reply back without speaking. Are you ready?" said Emeralda

"I am! I want to learn my own language to be able to communicate with everyone at the party!" Ruby replied in excitement

You could see the waves forming in Emeralda's brain and being sent through the air to Ruby; Ruby on the other hand seemed troubled. Her face was all red, as she tried hard to focus.

"You need to clear your mind to receive" Emeralda advised

The waves circulated Ruby's head and, as she finally relaxed, the waves penetrated her brain and she received the message.

"You can do it' That was your message, wasn't it?" Ruby asked

"Yes, good job! Now let's try you, to send me a message. Focus on the message and seeing the wave leaving your head and pushing it in the air to find me. You can also send images, symbols, colors, anything!" Emeralda explained

After 15 minutes of trying, Ruby finally managed to send the message 'I love you' to Emeralda. Ruby was now on another frequency level of vibration.

"I have never felt so successful in my life!" she exclaimed with joy

"We aren't done yet!" said Emeralda "Now it is time to receive your space watch. You can learn all the symbols of the ancient language we still use. The clock is very high tech and made of crystal-clear quartz. It can be activated with your thoughts- you don't have to press anything. The watch is connected to your nervous system so it projects the symbols you need into your mind! Moreover, the watch connects you to other beings in the Galaxy! Here you are, give it a go!"

Ruby activated the crystal watch with her thoughts and all the symbols were projected in the mind as well as swirling over her wrist.

"Thank you, Emeralda" said Ruby "This is incredible! I want to learn all of them! My very own portable Galactic Translator!"

"Well, there are a lot of presents and new information! But why is everyone so excited to see me?" Ruby asked

"Let me show you why!" said Emeralda.

Emeralda brought Ruby far away from the Castle, behind the queen's gardens; it was all misty and a black fog was covering the ground. A thin wall was the only thing separating what she just enjoyed in the castle and what she was witnessing now. This was a place once full of joy and life but was now abandoned; the ground poisoned and all the crystals dead.

"But why Emeralda?" Ruby asked

"Whatever you do, do not touch the black crystals; their poison will drain your life force. As I mentioned before, we send planet Earth positive vibrations to raise the planet to 5th Dimension. Some agendas do not like it; they create more fear on earth; the crystals cannot handle the negativity and are poisoned absorbing it all. The crystals need to have time to recover and cleanse, but now even our Moonwell for cleaning the crystals is poisoned. The citizens from the town of Takira had to be moved closer to the castle, some even live in the castle to be saved from the poison. A lot of great Sirians died to save humanity. But we cannot risk more of our kind being poisoned: They are all happy to see you because you are our only hope." said Emeralda, with tears running down her face.

"I assume you have tried spells, manifestation? And our mother has tried everything?" said Ruby

"Mother tried every spell available on the Akashic chronicles, every symbol. We lost a lot of warriors trying to engrave the symbols into the crystals to restore balance. But it didn't work. What we do know is the location of the low frequency coming from Earth! We believe that once this frequency is cut, the city might have a chance to recover- with our help. It is not possible for us to go to Earth as our spacecraft are always shot down. We need you, you signed up for this, and now is the time!" said Emeralda

"Tell me what I need to do and you know I will!" said Ruby

"The location of the Black Onyx that is emitting this heavy frequency back to us is at St. Paul's Cathedral in London!" said Emeralda

"Shall I leave now? I'm ready"

"No" said Emeralda "Wait for the party to be over; you will have a cake and more presents- the fight can wait another day!"

Ruby wasn't really in the mood for celebrating now that she knew their home was under such threat. Emeralda brought Ruby back to the party as Celeste was starting to get worried. The crowd was cheering Ruby's name as a huge amethyst crystal cake arrived on the dance floor, on top of which seemed to be a crystal cross. Ruby turned to her mother and said:

"Mother, we don't eat cake, do we?" Ruby giggled.

"The cake is actually a spell; so it is an edible cake. But no, we do not need human food. If you wish to taste it- be my guest, but take the cross off the top - it's another gift for you" said Celeste

Ruby was keen to find out about the cross so she attempted to pull it out, without success, while Koral gave her a hand; lifting her up so she could reach. Finally she managed to grab the cross and pull it out in one go. To everyone's astonishment, it turned out to be a crystal sword. The cross was the handle. Everyone gasped at its beauty as the sword had Ruby's name engraved on it with rubies.

"I am speechless! Thank you, my Queen!" Ruby said graciously

"It is my honour, Ruby! Please call me, mother!" Celeste whispered

The Queen stood up from her throne and everyone fell silent.

"Dear fellow citizens" she began "Thank you, from the bottom of my heart, for coming here tonight to celebrate a new beginning in the Castle with the new member of our family. Now it is time to stay at home and recharge until further notice. The fog is inching closer to our walls; we need to take precautions."

The party was over. Everyone was sent back to their crystal homes. Just a few more pink dolphins and mermaid stragglers jumped in and out of the water on their way. On the surface, the Queen was happy; but inside she was very worried about life on Sirius B.

CHAPTER SEVEN

Deception

It wasn't long before Ruby descended to Earth to start her mission. She manifested a great crystal warrior outfit with spiky crystals on top of her shoulders and a shield to match her crystal sword and wand to protect her most vital organ; her heart. It was the 10th of December 2019 and the clock was striking thirteen. Ruby headed straight to St. Paul's Cathedral. Instead of opening the main door, she looked around for a smaller, hidden door so that she could catch them by surprise. After a while, she found what she was looking for. She pulled her selenite wand from her costume and cast her first spell:

"Aperta ianua" she commanded, from the latin for 'open door.'

The door opened onto a huge corridor. Icons hung from every wall and a red carpet lead to a very tall wooden door with a big black lion's head for a door knob. She opened this door onto a room filled with empty seats and a tribuna- the kind of thing you see on a Sunday at church- nothing suspicious. As she walked further she saw another corridor, and a stairway leading underneath the cathedral. Ruby was very keen to keep following the stairs as she could hear some voices coming from beneath her. She ended up in front of a room with an open door; Ruby bravely entered. What she found was awful. On a black onyx table in the middle of the room, people encircled a pregnant woman; ready to sacrifice her. They were chanting in Latin about how her spirit would be forever remembered for a greater cause.

"STOP!" Ruby said

The moment she spoke the 'people' shaped-shifted and were no longer human but nasty green reptilians, thirsty for blood and ready to kill. They seemed to know who she was, but were not even slightly afraid. They tried to kill the woman first, before going for Ruby. But because they needed energy to charge, Ruby was fast enough to cast a spell"

"Clypeus" (Shield) Ruby said

An energetic shield protected the woman. Now Ruby was ready to kill the shape-shifters. She drew her crystal sword and started running toward them, slaying one by one, then turning to cast spells as she swung her sword. The reptilians turned to dust as she slew them. The fight was long, but Ruby did not get tired. The reptilians used their claws and teeth to try and kill Ruby, so she decided to try something else:

"Nunc eieci te ad alium se orbem terrarum" Ruby chanted a spell with her selenite wand

Her wand burst forth with golden energy and created a portal to send all the reptilians left alive to another world. Ruby's clothes were ripped and she had a few scratches on her legs and face, but overall, it was a successful first mission. Ruby asked the pregnant woman her name.

"Elena" she said

"Thank you so much for saving me!"

"You are free to go." said Ruby, and handed Elena her clothes.

Ruby was alone with the black onyx ball sitting right next to her, in the middle of the table. Ruby was determined to destroy it- but she didn't have a clue how she was going to do it.

"Solvo Onycso" Ruby said, commanding the onyx to destroy itself.

But the spell was useless. She tried a couple more but they didn't work either. Then she remembered something: She thought of the watch; and it started projecting the Sirian symbols in her mind. She took her wand and engraved the Onyx with one of the symbols. A small circle with three spider-like legs, angled like a clock: Transform.

As she engraved the symbol into the black stone, Ruby focused her mental force; directing the transformation of the crystal into dust.

What Ruby did not expect was to have a vision while she was engraving. But the message was loud and clear in her head. The moment she finished, the onyx started dissolving into a bright light, turning to dust in her hands. She smiled, almost laughing at her confidence and ability.

It was then that she saw a hole under the already destroyed onyx. She pressed it with curiosity, and a stairway leading downward unfolded. Ruby followed the path; it led to an endless tunnel. It was dark and moist. There was no noise and no sign of a single soul. Ruby used her sword to cast a light. She walked for about half an hour before finally starting to see something at the end of the underground tunnel. What she saw was shocking, so she made sure to cast her light out and only watch with her interdimensional senses. She scanned it with her 3rd eye vision and discovered an entire underground city, crowded with what looked like different kinds of reptilian. In the middle of the ground, there was a machine of light; as the reptile creatures entered it, they transformed into humans. The light would then shoot them upwards to the Earth world above. The underground city was full of children in cages as they were feeding off their innocence and fear. This was the root of pedophilia and black tantra magic being cast to Earth's energy field. Ruby realised that she was in the nest of hell, and she needed to get out as soon as possible; there were too many of them for her to fight alone right now. So for now, Ruby made her way outside to sit in the sun and recharge, before heading back up to Sirius B to deliver the good; and bad; news.

Now it all made sense, they had been living among us for centuries, controlling the media and the world as we perceive it to suit their agenda. I am going to bring an end to this and send them back to hell! Ruby thought to herself.

Ruby was crystallizing on Sirius B.

"Emeralda, Emeralda where are you?" Ruby yelled in the crystal garden.

She couldn't find anyone outside, so she approached the castle. As she was climbing the stairs to the main entrance, the gate opened. Emeralda came running down.

"Thank the crystals, you are safe and sound! I am so happy to see you! Look at your clothes! How about you manifest something better..." Emeralda smiled

"I have no time for fashion, Emeralda! Where is our mother?" Ruby asked

"She has been acting very strangely lately. She was furious today. I have never seen that side of her. Then all of a sudden she goes back to normal." Emeralda said

Ruby and Emeralda continued talking as they approached

their mother's bedroom, which was on the top floor of the castle so she could oversee everything below.

Ruby opened the door with her mind. Her mother was standing on the balcony. As Celeste turned to come inside, Ruby created an energetic chain to imprison her. A telepathic conversation followed:

"Where is my mother?!" Ruby screamed at Celeste

"What are you doing?" Emeralda nudged Ruby, confused.

Celeste is deceptive, her behaviour became stranger and stranger, as one of her eyes turned from blue to black.

"Celeste gave the command to all crystals in Takka to destroy themselves, Emeralda!" said Ruby "The crystals are starting to lose their power and are emitting a frequency of destruction instead of healing- by the power of the Queen. The Crystal citizens can no longer recharge from the crystals and Planet Earth has stopped receiving the healing energies needed for their ascension to the 5th dimension. Great plan, now tell me why did you give them the onyx?" Ruby turned on Celeste

"Is this true, mother?" Emeralda said angrily

"No, of course not my child. They have plenty of black onyx on Earth, why would they need ours!" Celeste responded calmly

"Alright." said Ruby "Could you explain then why no earthly bound spells were able to destroy it? The onyx was only destroyed by me engraving the Sirian symbol of transformation. I saw the vision of you handing them the onyx, I sensed your energy on it. Do not lie"

Ruby edged closer to the being, trying to be polite, when all of a sudden, she pulled her sword and stabbed Celeste straight into her heart! The being shapeshifted, and turned into dust.

"Look Ruby!" said Emeralda. The fog started lifting from Tikka city and slowly disappeared. "You saved the city just like the prophecy said. It will take some time for the crystals to restore before we bring back the citizens, but... wow! That was amazing! Ruby, I am so proud of the courageous warrior you have become. But we need to find our mother."

"And we will Emeralda, but now the world needs us! I found their nest, we will strike soon."

Ruby and Emeralda stood frozen for a bit. Then Emeralda suggested checking the Akashic Records for a solution. Ruby agreed. As they walked over the tower, Ruby manifested herself a new warrior outfit. Emeralda shot her a look.

"What?" Ruby giggled "I just want to look good for my next fight!"

Once they reached the tower, they placed their hands over the crystal and started to look for Celeste. Instead of finding Celeste, they found something mind blowing. A new pandemic had just been released on Earth, threatening to kill millions of innocent people. The virus was going to spread fast. Reptilians were regrouping for their final strike on human kind. The virus was made to distort the human DNA, to suppress people before they remembered who they are and what their mission is. Reptilians fear human ascension as they know we are stronger than them. Ruby agreed to descend to Earth to see what is going on, while Emeralda continued to look for their mother.

It was the most wonderful time of the year. Snow was tumbling onto the ground and Christmas and New Year were just around the corner. Ruby was planning to spend the holidays in Rashid's arms, on a road trip around Holland.

"Buzz..buzz..buzz" Ruby's phone rang

"Hi, Ruby it has been a while! I knew you would not call back so I decided to invite you for Christmas holiday here with me and my girlfriend in Spain. Would you like to join us? I can buy a ticket today?" came George's voice

"No, dad. Thank you for the offer. I've got other plans. You never accepted my relationship with Rashid, but my mum did."

"I just don't want to see you hurt." her father protested "Do what you want- just don't complain to me when it all falls apart. Have a great holiday, honey. I hope I see you soon."

Ruby hung up the phone and smiled. She felt like the biggest war had just been won. Matters of the heart were so special to her as a Sirian being; love is what governs Sirian's entire world, and can be the most creative; and the most destructive, force.

Ruby and Rashid spent the holidays in a very small village outside Amsterdam where they enjoyed some ice skating. But they did not need much entertainment to be happy together. Just being a couple was intoxicating enough; making love all day, spending time in the maze of the Den Haar Castle; a fairytale come true.

The night came for them to celebrate the New Year of 2020, fireworks brightening the sky. They raised their glasses of champagne, toasting a new beginning and Rashid said:

"I love you Ruby!"

After a year together, this was the first time he was able to express his emotions fully.

"I have loved you for so long, I just couldn't say it. The words stuck in my throat. Every time I was about to say it, I'd get too emotional and I couldn't deal with it. You have been very patient with me, nourishing our relationship. Thank you for all your patience and love while I have been cold to you. Believe me it is not on purpose, when I fall into a depression, I just can't feel much. Sometimes I even wonder why would you choose to be with me as I can't live up to your expectations. You have always been the bright sunlight in my day; I always look forward to seeing you. I feel I can open up and share my true self with you; no masks. You've shown me acceptance since day one, and I really appreciate it. I want you to know that you have changed my life in a very positive way. You believed in me when no one else did. I am not used to getting help, but you showed me it is better to trust and open your heart!" Rashid gazed into Ruby's eyes

"I never thought this moment would actually come. I never thought you would recognize me and express your love." Ruby smiled, brushing tears of joy from her face. "I have waited for so long; you breaking up with me so many times and getting back together has had some impact on my heart- but it never changed my feelings for you. I knew you were my soulmate; I knew the first time we met. Some say love at first sight; I call it karma from many lifetimes before. Oh, and good news... I even managed to get my father's blessing, so now nothing stands between us, from my side..."

Rashid could not say the same; his mother was still hesitant to accept Ruby, even though she gave her a scarf for Christmas. Ruby also felt more things have been hidden from her, but didn't want to spoil this moment. Ruby and Rashid kissed and made love until the sun came up! Ruby was full of love and at the peak of her happiness, but at the back of her mind she knew what was coming for humanity, and that her Sirius mother was still missing.

Ruby left again after having a wonderful time bonding with Rashid, and once again the distance between them was too much to bear.

CHAPTER EIGHT

Cosmic Battle

Ruby crystallizing on Sirius B

Written in the stars millions miles away, the ground for the 6th race was about to come to life. Galactic war was started on the astral plane as the Earth was suffering a pandemic crisis.

"Emeralda did you find anything in the Akashic Records?" asked Ruby

"Yes" said Emeralda "We know she is alive. I can still sense her energy and I am very close to finding where she is located.

Ruby, everything is energy, nothing is solid even if it looks like it. Everything you see in the media is polluted, no one will tell you the whole truth. Rich and famous people have their own agenda. You need to understand how things work on Earth. To become famous and rich you need to literally sell your soul-people sign a contract to have a reptilian being to possess them and rule over their soul. This is how reptilians get power, money and control. They have been ruling over humanity for decades, since Annunaki times. Reptilians were never supposed to stay and interfere with human kind as they are doing now, but the veil is lifting; they will no longer be able to mask themselves as humans. The moment we shift to 5D, their tricks will not work- humans will be able to see their true nature with the naked eye. At the moment only people with their third eye open can really sense and see them. Once you understand that everything is energy, you will learn how to bend reality and manifest it for the greater good of humanity. At the moment humankind is starting to understand that nothing is concrete. Their jobs and the economy are not solid, their families whom they have taken for granted for so long are the most valuable asset they have and planet Earth is cleansing after so much pollution. Anger and fear are rising at a low frequency, where love should have been instead. You need to understand all of this to be able to operate during this transformational time. Social isolation will bring people into depression and cause even more anxiety than being in a social environment. They are doing this for a reason; to crush people's spirit and to show power over humankind. But, people will start waking up to the problems of humanity. For example, eating meat- it's not only bad for the environment but bad for their human bodies, or 'Temples' as we call them. People need to understand animals also have feelings and carry a soul. A mother duck can die from a heart attack if her eggs are missing- the same way a mother would, if her child was kidnapped. They were never meant to be eaten by humans. Fruits, vegetables and nuts are a good food for a human soul. Meat is more traditional to reptilians and lower entities. As long as humans eat animals, their energy levels will be low and they will never ascend to a higher plane where animals and humans live in peace. It's true what they say- 'You are what you eat' -the reason is, you become an animal and stay only on the energy of the first chakra, not developing the rest. Sooner or later this chakra's energy gets depleted and you end up with an imbalance. The human body is a highly intelligent vehicle that can heal itself. Humans have lost touch with their ancient knowledge about how to heal their body, mind and spirit. This is your task- to remind them of their true power. Only when everyone is awake to the agenda presenting itself now, will they be able to shred and ascend to a higher plane, like you have. You must not hate the negative agenda; it is there for a reason. Actually, behind their negative impact they are highly evolved beings that dream of going back to their world. They cannot stand being on Earth; but they also have a mission. Planet Earth still lives in duality and someone has to serve the other side of the coin; they hope that after being through so many hardships, humanity will one day wake up. Your mission is to help humanity raise their consciousness through education, but not in the traditional way. Humans need to eat more healthily; teach them the essentials; all the ancient knowledge that has long been forgotten. There is no difference between a dog being burned alive for food and a cow being slaughtered on a farm. Both deserved to live and die in a natural cycle- untouched by human's animal behaviours. A structure of financial freedom is needed; people have been imprisoned by money for way too long. Most of the population live on the cusp of poverty while only a small percentage of rich people control the world. It is time to flip the pyramid upside down: Give the power back to the masses. If humans continue to be slaves, human life will become shorter and shorter- the body was never designed for so much hardship. It is your mission to teach humanity how to do it the right way, build new paradigms and do it for all. It is a hard task, but never impossible; with the right training you will be ready to strike. You need to make a plan. How do you want to create this? I am giving you full freedom- it's your baby; your project. Let me know when you are ready and we will discuss everything. Be aware, you manifest very fast- so watch out for what you think constantly. Kids are generally very attuned to our plane but they are very easy targets, absorbing the wrong information during childhood on Earth. Your goal will be to create an institute for where like-minded children can communicate and learn, to create a better future. Spiritual parents will be happy to have a place where their kids will feel accepted and understood. You will find your associate soon, his name is Mellow, he is from the fallen city of Atlantis. The age of Aquarius is here, it started in 2012 and it is your age Ruby; all the planets in your natal chart fall into the 11th house of Aquarius. Now is your time to shine. The Uranus/Neptune in conjunction in 1992 is connected to tearing apart old structures that no longer serve humanity, and building new ones for the greater good. This was the gateway; when your soul split from mine and entered the Earth plane."

Ruby had already been working on this manifestation with Celeste and decided not to ask how Emeralda knew about her idea as she was sure she'd been sending this information for a long time.

But she was so sad as in her heart. Rashid was still there and she missed him a lot, especially with the pandemic preventing them from seeing each other.

"My heart is constantly torn between love and career, it's a constant battle. You see on planet Earth, the mind is always ready for work, but the emotion of Love never follows the same rules. I am starting to realise that I need him in my life more than ever" said Ruby, confessing her pain to Emeralda

"Love is the most precious gift we are given in our lives. You must be wise and remember that. You will always be able to find a job and make a living; but you are not here to do a small job; you are here for something bigger than you can understand. I am sure it will all work out in the end" said Emeralda with a smile

"Thank you...You sound like our mother! Keep on looking for her- you know how to reach me if you have any news" said Ruby, and de-crystallized from Sirius B.

———————◁◆▷———————

March 2020

The world is in panic mode as the virus spreads to every part of the globe. Ruby's phone is buzzing.

Rashid spoke:

"Hello Ruby, I need to confess something to you. I have been thinking a lot about our last breakup and I realise it was partially my fault. I have been numb for so long; I was never completely there when you were pouring out your heart to me. I really regret that. I wish I'd responded to your love with love. But now I understand what love is. I am in love with you Ruby. I have been the whole time, I was just too afraid to admit it, first to myself- and then to you- because I was afraid of being hurt. But over the past year, you broke the shell and showed me that a depressed guy with type 1 diabetes can also be loved, and show love. You've helped me see past religion and I know now that I can't live without you, Ruby. I even wrote a poem for that specific day of the month to soothe your pain.

Patch on the Wound

This pain in your belly will go away.
It hurts but it's not here to stay.
I'm writing these words for you to cope.
And remind you to still feel the hope.
See I suffer when you do you know.
Just like Juliet did with Romeo.
Know that I love you though.
We might have our differences.
And struggle because of the distances.
But we'll manage, and we'll get there.
I want you to be here, not elsewhere.
Just hang in there, and push it through.
I'll be with you.
Know that's the truth.
Hope that it's soon.
This afternoon?
Too good to be true.

"Wow, did the pandemic get to you or what?" joked Ruby, crying with happiness. "I never thought we would see each other again even over the phone and to be honest, I had lost hope of us being together at all." Ruby was ecstatic

"I want you to move here and live with me in Amsterdam so we can be together" Rashid proposed

Ruby's mouth was not moving, but in her head, she was screaming.

Another dilemma! How was all this going to be possible, especially in the middle of a pandemic. She'd have to find a job, learn a new language, start over again when the world was not moving. Fear started to take hold. Her heart was beating faster and faster, blood rushing to her head.

"Rashid that is a great idea" she said "But we need to plan everything. Like where I am going to stay? And what about work? - I am about to receive my shares from the company - if I leave this year I will lose them. And that could be a down payment for a house together. We need to really plan this."

"I agree with you Ruby" he said "There is a lot to be planned and I know it's a lot to ask of you. I know I would never move like this; I always calculate everything. I would understand if you wanted to stay in London, but this distance is killing us. I don't know how much longer I can hold on. Life is happening around me, you know, now I'm not depressed I go skating every day in the park.. there are girls interested in me but I don't pay any attention to them, because of you."

Ruby took a deep breath. "I want to share something with you I never shared before." she said "When I arrived in the USA for the last year of uni, I actually moved to live in Maine because of someone I loved at the time. We also had a long-distance relationship and he wanted me to go and live with him. So I planned everything, I paid my program to apply for a job and I was there! From the beginning, it was terrible. I arrived and everything promised, like having an apartment already set up for us, was not true. We lived in a shared house with 5 other people and ended up going to live with his parents to save money. My visa was already expiring so I was thinking of ways I could stay to be with him so I applied for a college which cost me £14,000 per year- just to extend my visa and be able to stay in the relationship. His mum didn't even wait for my documents to arrive; she just wanted me out of the house; didn't want immigrants under her roof. Everything I had I invested in this relationship; all my money, sacrificing my family and friends in Bulgaria to move to the USA- for what? To be thrown out on the street with all my suitcases in the rain. He even took my car away and just stayed at his mum's. So now as you are asking me this, I wonder if you are able to help me set myself up there, or you are just expecting to wake up one day and I magically live in Holland and have everything sorted. Think about that and we'll talk again." Ruby's heart was racing but she knew it was right to tell Rashid about her reservations.

By the next day Ruby had already applied for an online Dutch course and two jobs in Amsterdam. She was excited to share the news with Rashid:

"Good morning babe, I just wanted to talk to you about my progress with the idea of moving and share something special- I already applied for a job and a course and talked to my boss about the move..." Ruby said

"Good morning Ruby." said Rashid quietly "I have thought very hard about it, and I think we should part ways and look for love closer to us. I don't think I can put all that energy into you moving here. If you lived here it would be another story but now, with the pandemic, I think it is best for us to move on.

For a moment, the year flashed in front of Ruby's eyes, all at once. The times he was depressed and she was there for him, their time on the beach, dancing together, enjoying life together. Everything shattered in a second.

Her smile hid itself deep and her heart turned from a ball of hot desire, to ice. Love comes and goes with the blink of an eye; you need to catch the moment. Always so sudden, unexpected.

Who is going to catch you when you are falling in the abyss? voices in her head

Ruby hung up the phone with her last strength, and burst in tears. Ruby took a pen and wrote as the tears were falling on her cheeks.

A poem your will never read:

It is my love's birthday today
And I am so far away
To be with him is my desire
In his arms to ignite the fire.
He is not ready to be with me just yet
As he wishes to be alone and find his way
I must step aside and let it be
Even though my heart screams the opposite
One day we may reunite
Understanding what we want from life.
My love for him goes deep within my heart
That is where I keep my precious memories
It seems like yesterday when I saw your eyes at first
But no it's been a year now and I feel you close
I hate goodbyes he knows that too
So I would just say I will see you soon
I hope you have a great birthday today
As I am wishing you the best hoping one day
You will be ready for my love!
I know the lows make you feel asleep
But don't you worry I am always here to love you deep
Even when we are apart
You are always in my heart
The virus won't break us apart
Because our love is better than art.
I hope you dream of me
Pouring my love like a honeybee.
This poem hope to bring you a smile
Like a sweet tea of chamomile.

Suddenly, a ball of light came though Ruby's window. It whispered.... 'TOUCH ME. TOUCH ME.'

Ruby stretched out her hand and the moment it touched the light, she transcended another dimension.

"Where am I? Hello! Anybody here?"

"You are beyond the 6 dimension, where we don't have male or female; every soul joins the many to become ONE." came a voice from the abyss "You are in the infinite-possibilities-playground! Here, love is part of life. No one goes looking for love like they do on Earth. You have come here to complete one big lesson:

Love is in you, you learned self-love and self-worth. This is an important part of your journey. See, here everything is made of loving energy, but when you're on earth and you have something beautiful like your connection with Rashid, Angels will always test your love to see if it is strong enough to survive the harsh challenges of life. Life as you know it will soon vanish and you will need to be strong, you will need to be a warrior"

Ruby started to panic. Where was that voice coming from? Why was everything so bright? It looked like another galaxy. She felt everything was connected- it vibrated in her core. Why wasn't she with a body? Was she dead?

"Ruby, I am what you call God- the infinite Creator. I hear all the pain, but the pain of an aching heart is always loudest. You believe in Love without borders. Religions love separate gods and portray things to suit their agenda, but you see through the veil; you see people's hearts are not where they come from or what they have or what they believe in. It takes a very strong character to be able to stand that alone" said the voice, answering the questions in her head. "There's something I would like to share with you, as I feel your pain is about a man: The key to waking men up is found within a sacred union- you rebirth him. A process in which a woman stops having sex with a man for a period of time; while loving him fiercely with all her heart; until he awakens and she feels his heart-opening. Will he stay? Will he show up? Will he choose to love? In your case, he decides to leave and that is alright Ruby. If you keep giving your energy to men that have not matured, they will never learn to grow up. Remember, he won't make it on his own as a single man. He needs to be in the physical presence of the womb. He won't know the way. He has to trust his woman and follow her feminine ways. The trust is important because she won't have answers to soothe his masculine mind... he will want to know why? For how long? To what end? He can't understand. You will just have a knowing, a deep feeling that you can't explain or put into words. Listen to the deeper knowing from your heart, your womb and your yoni's call for only the purity of your beloved to enter your most sacred space. Sometimes you have to say no, so you can go into the healing of your past sexual wounds and traumas in this life, in past lives and those of the collective. Before his heart opens he will first need to welcome all his feelings to come up... he must learn to sit with them, to be with them. To own them. All these feelings of anger, of conditioning consciousness; both within and collectively; of fear of abandonment, fear of commitment and entitlement to have his needs met by women. The justifications for getting his needs met will make him want to leave.

He will tell himself that you are not choosing love, as he wants you to move there to meet all his emotional and sexual needs. He will tell himself that he is loving, that he supports you, but in reality, he needs to heal the inner little boy inside. He is a physically grown man. But emotionally a little boy. He is scary. Unpredictable. Can't be trusted; his emotions are fluctuating very fast and nothing concrete will come of it unless he realises what he wants from life and heals his inner child. Work on raising your Kundalini energy up as you attract your soul mate. That would be the way to produce angelic children if you wish to have a family full of love. Ruby, if you ever hear the words *you owe me'* or *'your body is mine'*- run and never look back. My creations are different, but they need to be treated with respect-no one ever owns anyone! You were born a free spirit to experience human life and will come back to me as a free spirit! Try not to hold too much trauma as you will have to go and heal before you decide to go back to Earth if you decide at all. The true separation from the feminine is his most painful wound. He must learn to take care of himself, to nurture himself; not by self-pleasuring and finding other addictive behaviors to suppress these feelings; but by welcoming these feelings into his body and feeling them fully. Walking in nature, exercising, eating well and finding someone to talk to and be supported by. He will awaken only by taking responsibility for his maturity and understanding that this is the only process that will allow him to develop emotionally, in a way that heals the divide between the masculine and the feminine. The only thing that can bring him peace of mind is knowing: He is showing up in love for you at the same time as honoring his own spiritual karmic healing growth path and becoming a mature, emotional awakened man."

The moment the voice stopped Ruby seized something in the distance. As she approached it, the image started to appear. It was a big diamond-encrusted, golden cup filled with crystal water. Voices were calling Ruby to look into the cup. She gazed in but didn't see anything, but a reflection.

Then a force of nature came up and put her head into the cup. She started seeing the infinite possibilities of how her life could have developed and how it could still unfold.

"Choose me, choose me" the voices whispered.

Ruby saw something, but blinked and all of it vanished. When she woke up again in her bed, she still had tears on her cheeks.

She put her selenite wand on her forehead and transcended to Sirius B.

"Hey Ruby, what's wrong? Why are you crying?" Emeralda asked

"Emeralda I need to see that crystal bed again, I need some memories erased! My heart can't take it anymore" Ruby said desperately

"You know there is no going back, Ruby? Are you sure?" said Emeralda

"Yes." she said

Emeralda brought Ruby to the healing room where the crystalline bed was. The bed looked like a seashell that opened and closed, it was made of different crystals- mainly amethyst and crystal quartz. Before Emeralda closed the bed she said:

"Just say what you want to be removed. The crystals will absorb it for you. You should know that sometimes the crystals transmit information back as well."

Emeralda closed the bed.

Ruby kept her eyes closed because the shimmering of the crystals was very strong. She heard some very pleasant voices calming her while the process took place. The crystals started emitting light, penetrating her skin to the cellular level. Ruby commanded what she wanted to be removed; her heart was aching too much.

"Process complete" the voice of the bed said.

Emeralda opened the bed and helped Ruby up.

"How do you feel Ruby? Any signs of lightheadedness?" Emeralda asked

"I am experiencing feelings I have never felt before. I feel so alive. I am a warrior and everything is crystal clear now." Ruby's eyes widened as she absorbed the abundance of light and information.

"Ruby, you look even different. Your facial expression is younger, you are more physically toned, your green eyes and hair color are brighter. I can see your healing session went well, but you need to rest now. Let me help you get back to Earth" Emeralda said

"No, I need to find the Moldavite. Where is it? Tell me?" Ruby insisted

"What moldavite, Ruby? What are you talking about? Did you receive some information from above? Emeralda asked
"Yes, I need to find the Moldavite to complete my mission on Earth, where is it?" Ruby asked again

"I only know of one Moldavite. It is hidden deep in a Rainbow Cave at the end of the Crystal Forest. Mother never let me study that crystal, she told me it wasn't time." Emeralda replied "Ruby I can take you to the cave, but you have to know that not a lot of citizens have come back alive after going in. Some say the Moldavite is too strong for some bodies and maybe especially strong for your earth body."

"I understand." said Ruby calmly "Believe me, I know what I am doing more than I ever have in my life. You always talk about mother- what about our father? Can you tell me anything about him?"

"Our father, Elhun, was part of the Galactic Warriors, he was sworn to protect the galaxy and was always sent on missions. One time he went to fight the Titans, and he never returned. Mother tried everything to find him, but there was no trace. He was a great father, full of love in his heart, and a brave soldier." Emeralda sent her memories of him telepathically so Ruby could see and feel them.

Emeralda knew that the forest was far away and they would waste a lot of time walking, so she suggested that the crystal cats fly to the entrance. Ruby loved cats and had one on earth. She knew that a bond would be important for a smooth ride, so she stood for a moment in front of the crystal cat and drew an Om symbol on its forehead. The cat bowed down to Ruby so they can both climb on. The cat spread its wings wide open, and flew.

"Emeralda, I am not complaining or anything, but I miss my furry cat" Ruby giggled

"I love your jokes or shall I say my jokes? Hahaha. You will get used to it. Crystal cats are amazing creatures. Now you've bonded with it, it will serve you forever- unless you decide to give it's freedom!" laughed Emeralda

They flew to the entrance and left the cat waiting next to a tree. This forest was like nothing you have ever seen. Every tree was multicoloured and made of different kinds of crystal, sending different energies into the air so when you breathe, you recharge so much you want to fly instead of walk. The sky was crystal clear with no clouds at all. It was so peaceful, you could only hear a water fountain nearby, and the sound of fairies flying around. But as they came closer they heard strange noises coming from the fountain. They sounded like screams.

"Emeralda, can you hear that noise? What is it? It sounds terrifying." said Ruby

"This is the fountain of life, Ruby. This is where souls that have just died from lower dimensions come back to our city to heal before they start another journey." said Emeralda

"So this is like a graveyard on Earth? Sounds like it anyway." said Ruby

"Where there is death, there is life! They are not dead at all, they are merely starting again and seeing what they have accomplished during their lives on other planets" Emeralda replied.

Ruby sensed a vibration in the leaves. The sound increased as wind came howling up from the darkness. All of a sudden, a floating, bluish-silver, glowing energy showed up. The energy was calm and comforting. The being looked like a female with a petite figure and a glowing tattoo on her forehead in the symbol of a pyramid. The same symbol you see on the dollar bill. Her eyes were sparkling blue; reflective, pearlescent. The crystal ball staff she held had some kind of advanced technology that could help clear out thoughts and emotions; confusion, contraction. Other beings approached and joined the conversation.

"Who are you?" the being asked

"We are the Crystal Palace Princesses, Ruby and Emeralda.

Who are you? 'Emeralda asked

"I am Ania, I come from Andromeda. We have never seen a human set foot on our sacred ground before. What are you seeking here? You have no rights to our land. The Rainbow Cave does not belong to the Crystal Queen." she whispered as more beings approached.

"We are looking for the Moldavite crystal. I need it, and I need it now- do you know where I can find it?" Ruby yelled

"We are the Guardians; we keep the crystal safe. We have been keeping it safe for an eternity, what would you need it for?!" The guardian asked, reaching out for her crystal staff and adopting a threatening position

"We want to save planet Earth and raise its frequency to the fifth dimension. I know from the Akashic Records that Andromedians are friends with Sirians. We live in peace together. We need your assistance." Ruby explained

After some careful negotiation, the Guardians decided to give Ruby part of the Moldavite - but not the whole crystal as that would be against their will and means of existence! They asked to be followed to the Rainbow Cave and that the princesses stay at the entrance. They couldn't see much as the guards would not allow them to peek, but even just the outside was spectacular. Vivid neon coloured energy-waves circled around the entrance; no wonder it was called the Rainbow Cave.

"Here, we give you part of the crystal; part of us. Use it wisely!" Ania said

They were kept in an isolating crystal box, to be neutralized and used only when open. The crystal's glowing bright green energy was so strong, it made you dizzy if you stared for too long.

"Thank you, it will be used for good intentions only" Ruby reassured them "Emeralda, I have to go now, but I will be back very soon I promise. Please get home safely. Take care of Enoa, my crystal cat"

Ruby put the selenite wand on her forehead and transcended to Earth with the Moldavite crystal.

"Bye Ruby. I will. I am always with you, remember that." Emeralda whispered

The next morning Ruby woke up very early and immediately called her mother:

"I am sorry I have been like a ghost for the past few months and we haven't had a chance to speak much, but I have been very busy with work and now more than ever I can see what I am destined for."

"It's so nice to hear your voice. My heart has been waiting for so long! We are doing well; we spend most of our time working in the garden. Paskal says 'hi'-he always thinks of you. Are you coming home soon?" Anna asked

"No mum, this is what I wanted to discuss with you. I am not coming back home for a while. I'm sorry, I know it's hard to swallow." said Ruby

But the line had broken off as Ruby was speaking- her mother hadn't heard her.

"What you are thinking in your head is possible. Do it!" whispered Emeralda, communicating telepathically

Ruby did not want to tell her mother there was a chance of her never coming back, so she came to a decision to do something called bi-location from Sirius B. This meant she could exist in two places simultaneously. Ruby learned a lot from the Akashic Records and she was confident to perform the spell:

"Ano-RA for-kha-run charon" she chanted in Sirian.

As she was chanting and making a magic spell with her wand, another being started crystallizing next to her; an exact copy of Ruby.

"Hello, me!" said Ruby to her bi-location self "You know where to go; you will feel me calling you back when I need you."

The clone left and Ruby called her mother again to let her know she was coming home safe and sound right now and she would stay until the virus crisis was over. Ruby had to focus on her big mission. Now that there was no boyfriend to distract her and her earthly family was content, she could make the next move.

All the ingredients were ready and she left a quick note on her nightstand just incase:

Today we must make a difference in the world around us. For you, the one that never closed your heart and no matter the loss, continued to love. Love is the only way home. Tonight I will plant the greatest combination of crystals: In the heart of London, at 11:11 a new beginning is to be set in stone. For you, who dares to love, to seek inside yourself for answers- I am giving you this gift!

Love,
Ruby

Ruby crystallised with all the crystals needed in Trafalgar square with one touch of her wand. The streets were empty. The fear spread by the media about the virus killing people by causing lung damage was seeded into every human being. But staying home was definitely not a solution. Ruby positioned herself in the middle of the square. She put the Ruby, Moldavite and the Emerald on the ground for a moment to get ready.

She pulled the selenatine wand and activated her Om tattoo to start the channeling process. At that moment a portal in the sky opened and a golden beam of energy slowly started shooting down to her crown chakra, as Ruby placed the crystals. "By the power of Sirius given to me I command all the crystals to combine in the Flower of Light, now! The energy I draw from Sirius B is a healing energy that is going to be amplified to the most rural place on Earth and cause a huge transformation among the living!"

As Ruby was channeling, the crystals started to form a beautiful multi colored lotus flower, radiating healing rainbow energy.

In the Quantum Universe anything is possible. Just as Ruby was about to say the final activation code, a cat appeared next to her, carrying a message:
"Warning! Warning! The combination of crystals is fatal for the human body, would you like to proceed?"

Ruby was determined not to wait a second longer, she had to help Planet Earth accelerate it's an evolutionary process to the 5th Dimension.

She put her right hand over the lotus to activate it and chanted:

"Yuthawa" sending universal love to flow over humanity

A huge energy wave lifted Ruby in the air and threw her aside. It ripped her clothes and left her unconscious. The frequency of the 5th Dimensional energy was so high that it disengaged the reptilian DNA in every human, bringing a sense of freedom. The laser of golden energy penetrated the core of earth, destroying all the underground tunnels of hidden reptilian entities. The fear of pandemic was lifted as the energy made its way with a ripple effect all over the globe, out to the most rural places on Earth. People started to feel different, more vibrant, more alive, happy to go outside and enjoy the abundant life they were born to live. The heart chakra's energy was lifted to its highest peak, bringing healing, love and joy into people's hearts. The Moldavite's green energy soothed all the patients in the hospitals, dissolving the respiratory tract infections. People started to experience the 12 strands of DNA activation as nausea, headache and third eye pulsation were common signs of absorbing the new energy.

It was a great time for humanity; a time for celebration and bonding with other human beings and everything around them. A new relationship between humans and animals had formed and new teachings were starting to evolve. Life on Earth as we knew it, was over. No more pain and suffering... at least for now.

As she was battling on Earth, Angel warriors were battling reptilians in the astral plane. Many wars were in place to achieve one single goal- human freedom. All the cosmic beings were working very hard for this ascension sending high frequencies to Earth to fight the negative agenda that was terrified of losing its power of control and greed upon humanity."

CHAPTER NINE

Ascension

"Princess, we are starting to experience glitches in the Earth's matrix. The Planet's vibration has been boosted dramatically; the souls in the Fountain of Life have disappeared!" Koral shouted

Emeralda, who was charging on her bed, slowly opened her eyes and smiled.

"We did it!" she said "Send Alunkara to bring Ruby's unconscious body from Earth. We'll put her into a charging bed. We need to act fast; I sense her vital energy is diminishing."

"Right away Princess" said Koral

A light came down to earth and wrapped around Ruby's body, lifting her up into the spacecraft and gently placing her on a crystal quartz bed. While she was travelling through time and space, Emeralda kept herself busy setting up a party...

Three hours later, Emeralda opened the crystal bed. Ruby was regaining consciousness again; slowly opening one eye, and then the other. Emeralda helped her up.

"Congratulations Ruby, you did it! You saved the world! Now it is time to celebrate!" Emeralda said

"How come I am still alive?" said Ruby "I thought I was dying"

"You did die." Emeralda replied "Your ego dissolved and you broke off the wheel of the Karma cycle; learning and evolving from past galactic lessons. Your contract on Earth is now finished. You don't have to reincarnate anymore if you don't want to! As your parallel self it was a pleasure to work with you. I also learned a lot from you, Ruby."

"As a human it was my pleasure to save the world and make sure we can still exist in the future. Now, can you help me pick an outfit for this party?" Ruby smiled.

The Palace' garden was crowded with beings from all around the Galaxy. Most of the guests were blue Sirians, whose skin is perfectly smooth; it's not made of the same substance our bodies are. More like dolphins. Soft and sensitive; velvety. Their eyes have a gentle movement in them, like a solar corona around the pupils. Crystal cats played around with the Sirian, Andromedian, Pleiadians, Amphibian and Mermaids Kids. The merpeople were always present to celebrate the start of the Golden age's new beginning.

Ruby and Emeralda came down the stairs holding hands. Ruby was dressed in a long, sparkly, multicoloured crystal dress with her crystal sword on her waist. Her curly hair bounced up and down and she had a soft, joyful expression on her face. Emeralda wore her green emerald, mermaid-style crystal dress. She didn't have hair, but she wore her Emerald crown beautifully. As they came closer, everyone started clapping them for a job well done. The DJs were playing songs that were...hard to explain- they sounded a bit like Techno but softer and more transcendent. Everyone danced while the kids ran around with the cats in the garden.

"Ruby, come with me I would like to show you something" said Emeralda

Ruby followed Emeralda away from the crowd and the loud music.

"Look at the sky! Do you see all these energy traces?" Emeralda asked

"Yes, they are traces from spacecraft, right?" Ruby replied

"No, these are all the souls from the Fountain of Life that were released when you activated the code. They are all travelling back to Earth to start what we call the 6th race of human beings!"

Ruby was stunned; speechless and overjoyed at the same time. "You know what I am thinking, right Emeralda?"- Ruby smiled

"Let's go and find our mother." she said

Ruby and Emeralda left the party secretly while everyone was enjoying the new beginning. They knew their mother was alive and were determined to bring her back to Sirius B.

"Do you ever forget the person you love?" Rashid asked his friend Mo

"No, you just learn to live with the pain. It's like a splinter in your heart- it won't kill you; but it's always there." Mo replied
The radio was playing 'Diamonds' by Rhianna.

"This is Ruby's favorite song" said Rashid "I need to go. She was right- no religion, distance and language should ever get in the way of love. I just refused to see it. I need to go, Mo."

"Where are you going to go? You broke up with her...Are you mad?" said Mo

"I am going to drive to the UK and tell her how I feel. I hope it's not too late. This time I will propose!"

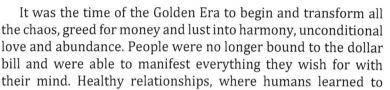

It was the time of the Golden Era to begin and transform all the chaos, greed for money and lust into harmony, unconditional love and abundance. People were no longer bound to the dollar bill and were able to manifest everything they wish for with their mind. Healthy relationships, where humans learned to make divine love connecting to the Cosmos and creating high frequencies children. Pollution and climate change was diminished and new technologies were implemented on Earth. Humans finally understood the concept-"We Are One".

It was the best of times,
It was the worst of times,
It was the age of Aquarius,
It was the age of heart and soul connection.

Never stop loving no matter how big the loss is, as love is the only way back home.

Ascension

To Be Continued .....

Dictionary

Here you will find the meaning of all the names of beings and crystals used in this book:

Aneltha- The Flower of Light
Ania- The Rock Guard
Elham- The Warrior
Elma- Destiny
The Charon- The Unifier
For-kha-run- The Symbiosis
Ano- RA For-kha-run Charon- The universal symbiosis unifier
Yuthawa- The Universal Love
Koral- Universe of the Man

Crystal names and their properties:

Moldavite: with its beautiful green energy, is first and foremost a stone of the heart. ... Green crystal energy is used to resolve blockages and to re-balance the Heart Chakra, helping us understand our own needs and emotions clearly. Clearing any respiratory system infections.

Ruby gemstones are effective psychic protection stones, and are excellent assets to help you to defend yourself against psychic attack from negative entities. They are powerful healing crystals for you to use as their vibration acts as a barrier against those who want to steal your energy. **Ruby** is a powerful heart stone, opening and activating the Heart chakra.

Celestite crystals are beneficial healing crystals for you to utilize to aid you to contact your guardian angels. They are a soft blue color and have a high vibration that is excellent to use in meditation. Their energy is both calming and uplifting, and will aid contact with angels.

Emerald - loyalty and provides for domestic bliss. It

enhances unconditional love, unity and promotes friendship. Keeps partnerships in balance and can signal unfaithfulness if it changes colour. It stimulates the heart chakra, having a healing effect on the emotions as well as the physical heart.

If you would like to contribute to the creation of
The Universal Wisdom Institute, please send an email
to tanya.dhadzhieva@gmail.com

Printed in Great Britain
by Amazon